# A ROLAND COLONNADE

DAVID BENTLEY HART

# A Roland Colonnade

Angelico Press

For information, address:
Angelico Press, Ltd.
169 Monitor St.
Brooklyn, NY 11222
www.angelicopress.com

ppr 979-8-89280-128-7
cloth 979-8-89280-129-4
ebook 979-8-89280-130-0

Book and cover design
by Michael Schrauzer

Dedicated to
the open hearted philosopher,
polymath,
and poet
Donald Patrick Bradley, Jr.
("Donnie")
1996–2025

"He's very gentle."

# CONTENTS

# INTRODUCTION

THIS IS NOT a sequel—but rather only a companion—to *Roland in Moonlight*. In fact, its first six chapters antedate that book, and all six of them were assumed into its pages in adapted and extended form. The purpose of this volume is simply to assemble an exhaustive collection of all the individual columns featuring Roland in their original states, for the sake of a complete record of that mighty soul's literary posterity, and as a tribute to someone I and my family loved and love immeasurably. Many of my readers, I should also note, have requested a chronicle of this kind. As will be evident from the repristinated texts, the whole series came about almost by accident; the first of them was originally intended to stand alone, generating no successors, and was written as a description of a dream rather than as an account of a real conversation occurring in some magical and privileged realm of receptive consciousness in between waking and dreaming states. That gradually changed in subsequent installments, and by the time *Roland in Moonlight* was written the full picture had largely emerged. I think that all along Roland was gently guiding me toward a clearer understanding of what was going on, as well as of the grander themes around which our moonlit encounters were constantly turning. One can certainly see how his sagacious counsels were planting seeds in my mind that in time would grow into fully realized books, not only the one that bears his name in its title, but also *That All Shall Be Saved* and *All Things Are Full of Gods* (and probably some others as well).

Those first six columns appeared originally in a print journal for which I used to write. There they served as entries in a regular feature created for me by the editors, the format of which obliged me to confine each of them to roughly 1,550 words. The later seven columns, however, appeared originally in my own online Substack publication *Leaves in the Wind*, which gave me the luxury of expanding them to more commodious dimensions, more consonant with the style of the book. The final five were written in a continuous fashion, mostly because I had a premonition that they would be the last of the series, and so I was reluctant to bring them to a close. This was not because Roland was exhibiting any noticeable signs of ill health; I was aware of his age—more than fourteen years, a goodly sum for a dog of around fifty pounds—but he was a vigorous fellow still. Rather, it was something about the expression on his face when my eyes met his as I was writing that gave me a sense that our time together in this life was nearing its end. I deal with his passing, though, in the Coda appended to this volume, so I will say no more about it here. Even those pages contain not the proper encomium he deserves, but only scattered reflections; I find that even now, seven months since losing him at the time of this writing, I simply do not have the emotional strength to say all I feel, or to try to say what my wife and son feel, about someone whose presence was pure joy to all of us.

Before closing, I should answer a question that readers have asked me repeatedly. Many have noticed that, when referring to Roland by his full name, I called him Roland W. Hart. What, many want to know, does the 'W' stand for? In fact, it stands for Wu—or, more precisely, Wù, or even 婺, which means Beauty. So, Roland 婺 Hart, though he occasionally liked to joke that another character — 霧, also pronounced Wù, meaning mist or fog — might be used instead, given how lost some of my conversations with him seemed to leave me, and given also how very deep the air of mystery was that always hung about us when we had our little colloquies together.

It seems somehow both as if an eternity has elapsed between our parting and now, and as if no time has passed at all. I imagine that will always be the case.

PART ONE

# THE ORIGINAL
# SIX COLUMNS

# 1

# Roland on Consciousness

A FEW MONTHS AGO, the morning before my eldest brother was to return home to Norway after a long visit, I dreamed that I had just awakened in the early light of dawn to find my dog Roland sitting at the end of my bed, a bar of softly glaucous shadow—cast by the central casement frame of my double window—draped over his shoulders like a prophet's mantle. Roland is of middling size, with a shorthaired coat of mottled white, brown, and black, and with a handsome face with a coal-black nose and deep brown eyes; and I recognized at once the profound melancholy in both his posture and his expression. "What's wrong?" I said, after a moment of uneasy silence.

He slowly shook his head, and then—in a voice plangent with sadness—replied, "I have to leave you. I have to go to Norway with your brother."

I was astonished. For one thing, I could not recall ever hearing Roland speak before, at least not this clearly; I certainly did not know he had a voice so much like Laurence Harvey's (though with a warmer, furrier tone). For another, he had given no indication before this of any intention of leaving us; and, given the depth of his attachment to my wife, the very notion would have been inconceivable to me. "Why?" I asked. "What do you mean?"

He sighed, bowed his head for a moment, then raised it again to look into my eyes with the frankest of gazes.

"Your brother and I knew each other long ago," he said. Then, seeing my bewilderment, he immediately added, "Oh, not in this life, of course. I'm only three years old, after all. In another life, very long ago, countless *kalpas* in the past, in a better age than this our present *Kali-yuga*. In those days, you see, I was a god in the *Tushita* heaven, and your brother was my little pet monkey T'ing-T'ing. We were quite inseparable." An amused smile appeared on Roland's face and he gave his head a gentle, obviously affectionate wag. "What a scamp he was. How often he would don a small chaplet of silver bells, clamber up onto the back of my throne of jade and gold, cavort in merry little capers above my head, and then suddenly tumble down into my lap. Even Maitreya and the goddess bodhisattva Guanyin couldn't help laughing, and the tender warmth of their mirth flowed down even into the deepest *narakas* and momentarily eased the torments of the damned."

"I had no idea," I said after a moment.

Roland was still lost in his memories, however. "Some of his antics were terribly mischievous, and I was often urged to exercise more discipline over him. But I couldn't—he delighted me so. On a few occasions, he raided the banqueting table of the gods before they'd seated themselves. Sometimes he stole flagons of wine and made himself drunk. Twice he slipped into the divine orchards and gorged himself on the peaches of celestial longevity. Once, when the demons of *Pratapana* mounted one of their pathetically futile escalades against the ramparts of the heavens, he sat high up on the walls pelting them with peach-stones and screeching with unseemly laughter. But I loved him so."

Here Roland paused to bite at an itch on his haunch and then to smooth his fur with his tongue.

"Anyway," he resumed, "our long idyll reached its end when each of us exhausted his stores of good karma, and we both plunged back down into the spawning-ditches of *punabbhava*, and into the tangled meshes of *pratitya-samutpada*...a humiliating, but inevitable, dégringolade. *Anitya*, you know. Thereafter our karmic paths diverged for aeons. But now we've found one another. How could we bear to be parted again?" And a lugubrious sigh escaped his lips. "Oh," he said, his manner suddenly brisker, "that black bear came back last night and got into the trash again."

"I thought I heard you barking at something..." I began.

"Yes, I saw him from the living room window. I caught a glimpse of gleaming ursine teeth in the moon-light and I'm afraid that, when I recognized what I was looking at, an atavistic thrill of pure terror set me off. Irrepressible canine instinct, I'm afraid. I'd help you clean up the debris, but I have no thumbs." He turned his head as if about to jump down from the bed, but then paused and turned back to me. "You know, that's a very potent word, really — recognized, I mean...recognition..."

"How so?"

"Well, I've been pondering the problem of consciousness a great deal lately, and how impossible it is to fit it into a truly mechanistic account of life or of evolution — I mean at the most elementary level. Take simple recognition of something, for example: there you have an instance of seemingly irreducible intentional consciousness, right? But we know what a thorn in the side of materialism intentionality is: it's a conspicuous example of final causality right there in the midst of supposedly aimless mechanical events...its content is eidetic...you know, dependent on mental images, and so on conscious thought...it supplies a specific, finite *meaning* to experience that the physical order can't provide.... Well, simply said, it doesn't fit into the mechanistic story, does it? And so, as I understand it, the really consistent materialist position is that consciousness and intentionality is all secondary, even illusory, the epiphenomenal residue of purely mechanical processes. Supposedly, if you delve down deeply enough — into the body's neural machinery or into the dark backward and abysm of evolutionary time — you'll find that all intentional activity dissolves into a series of unconscious, aimless physical functions, which natural selection has refined into such a complex order that it generates the illusion of unified conscious intention."

He paused to scratch the back of his ear with a hind paw, then resumed: "Take my silly fright at that bear's teeth. Allegedly that would be just a neural agitation that only seems to have a rational content and purpose — survival — but that's really just the fortuitous result of an accidental juxtaposition of physical effects, mechanically coordinated by evolution. If you could trace my instinctive fear back in time, you'd arrive at some primitive organism without eidetic consciousness or intentional awareness, in which just by chance the shape of a bared tooth would — for no *reason* — provoke the neural response of flight. And then, since this would accidentally have the salutary effect of helping preserve that organism's life, that neural tendency would be preserved and transformed over generations into an indurated genetic predisposition. Only later would the elaborate stage-trickery of consciousness arise out of all that biochemistry, like vapors from a swamp. Well, do you believe that? Could any mechanical coincidence that bizarrely pointless and rare ever be sufficiently specified by natural selection? Do you really think that that neural reaction could even have occurred without some kind of eidetic recognition — some formal idea — present?"

"Well…"

"Of course not," he continued. "These materialists say it's mechanism all the way up — or at least up to some inexact point where some kind of phylogenic or neural alchemy, which we hazily call 'emergence,' magically produces consciousness as a kind of tinsel party-crown atop the machine. Nonsense, I say. Nonsense! It's just the opposite: consciousness and intentionality go all the way *down*, in varying degrees but continuously. Really, consciousness is at the ground of everything — it *is* the ground. Oh, did you remember to pick up some of those rawhide treats I like? I want to put some in my luggage for the flight."

"Look," I said, "do you really have to go to Norway? They'll probably put you in quarantine for a month when you arrive. And you know how prissy Europeans get about long-term visits by foreign animals without visas."

Now an almost pitying expression appeared on his face. "I'm sorry, but I must. T'ing-T'ing needs me… for spiritual guidance."

Knowing my brother as I do, I could think of no further plausible demurral, so I said nothing, merely nodding my head in resignation.

"You know," Roland added, "this whole business of consciousness reminds me of something that occurred to me the other day regarding superposition."

"Sorry—regarding…?"

"Superposition. You know, the measurement problem, double-slit experiments, whether there's a collapse of the wave-function—I certainly think there is—all that sort of business. You see, it occurred to me…"

Just then, however, a shrill, intolerably raucous claxon sounded. In a moment, the entire scene had melted away and I found myself emerging from sleep, savagely groping for my abominable alarm clock.

To awaken from an interesting dream before it reaches its end is always irksome; but I have to admit that my chief emotion, once the mists in my mind had begun to evaporate, was relief. It was very good to know that Roland would not be leaving on the evening flight with my brother. It was comforting, moreover, to have my sense of normality restored: I have no cause to believe, for instance, that Roland is a Mahayana Buddhist, much less a quondam Taoist deity once enthroned in a syncretic Buddhist heaven. So I was at peace. My only real regret on rising from bed, and for several days thereafter, was that, in all likelihood, I should never now find out what it was my dog had wished to tell me about quantum mechanics.

2

# Roland in Moonlight

IN MY DREAM, I had just entered the sitting room of my house. It was still several hours before dawn, but music was quietly playing: I heard the last lines and fading chords of Schubert's "*Der Leiermann*," in the recent recording by Jonas Kaufmann, before silence fell. I was confused at first, but I soon spied my dog, Roland, sitting on the carpet in front of the large bay window seat, staring out into the night. A soft, pure lunar light, shredded by the pine branches outside the glass into long glistening ribbons of pale silvery blue, poured gently into the room and over his mottled fur of white, brindled brown, and cobalt gray, and for a few moments it almost seemed as if he were himself little more than a pattern of shadows and moonlight. The illusion vanished, however, when he turned his head and held me for an instant in the cool gleam of his eyes, before returning his gaze to the window. "I'm sorry," he said in that warmly resonant voice of his (so hauntingly similar to Laurence Harvey's), "did the singing rouse you? I thought I had the volume down low enough to disturb no one."

"I don't think it woke me," I said. "I really can't recall."

"I suppose it's inconsiderate of me," he said. "It's just that I have many things on my mind, and it's only during these hours that I can get time to myself, just to think about things. During the day, my time is so taken up with domestic responsibilities—playing those games of fetch you all love so, letting you scratch my stomach, and so on. In these watches after midnight, though, I can reflect on things."

A memory began to rise to the surface of my thoughts. "Yes," I said, "weren't you going…yes, weren't you going to Norway with my brother?"

"Oh, I changed my plans. I really can't leave Mama"—he meant my wife—"all alone with you lot. I'll visit your brother in the summer, with your mother. That's not what I was thinking about now." He sighed. "Do you like that recording?"

"It's gorgeous."

"It is, isn't it? I'm so used to the *Winterreise* being sung by a baritone, by Fischer-Dieskau especially, and that dark ghostly timbre his voice had; but here's this marvelous tenor singing it with every bit as much pathos and power and mystery…. It's a piece that never seems to loosen its grip on me. Now that I'm four and

my ears are more mature, and my heart wiser, it's more
entrancing than ever. I mean, how did Schubert do it,
the poor perishing ape? Such ineffable tenderness, such
dulcet resignation, so much...leave-taking. That last
*Lied* in particular. No other composer ever produced
that exquisite combination of shattering melancholy and
whimsical buoyancy. What to call it? Merry sorrow? No.
Tragic jauntiness? No, that's awful." He shook his head.
"It's unbearable but beautiful, whatever it is — sweet
nostalgia, under the shadow of death's wings. You just
know that when he wrote those songs he could hear
the angel drawing near. But that's how it often is. We
frequently know...more than we know...anticipate
more.... Like those wonderful elephants."

"I'm sorry," I said, "you've lost me."

Roland turned and then rose and trotted over to me,
wagging his tail. "I'd be happy to explain. But, first, do
you happen to have any of those lovely bacon treats
about you? I could do with a little something just now."

I brought three treats from the pantry, sat in the window seat, and tossed them to him one after another. He
devoured them quickly (and a little noisily, to be honest),
then sniffed and tentatively licked my fingertips, then
rolled onto his back so that I could rub his stomach, and
finally stretched, turned over, and sat up again.

"Thanks," he said. "One gets peckish. As for the elephants...well, there are many delightful stories about
those magnificent creatures, about their intelligence
and sensitivity, their capacity for devotion and grief,
and so on. But I was thinking of the day that Lawrence
Anthony — you know, the 'elephant whisperer' — died
in 2012 at his house on that huge South African game
preserve that's more than a day's journey in size, and the

herds of rogue elephants he had rescued and tended all arrived within a couple of hours to pay their respects… to mourn, I suppose. I think I read about that in one of your old *New Atlantis* issues. Amazing. They'd been away for well more than a year, and then there they were. How did they know? What summoned them across all that wilderness, so they could intone their subsonic threnodies?" He shook his head wonderingly. "How do souls reach out across the limits of time and space? There's just no end to the mysteries of spiritual beings." He paused, almost with a start, and looked into my eyes with an expression of faint suspicion. "You don't have any sympathies for the degenerate views of those fellows that deny that elephants are spiritual beings, with immortal souls, do you? Like traditionalist Thomists and whatnot?"

The question alarmed me. "Oh, absolutely not," I said emphatically.

"And…and…" His brow furrowed, his eyes narrowed. "And dogs?"

"Look," I said, trying not to take offense, "you've known me all your life. You must know that I believe all conscious beings possess spiritual natures and have spiritual destinies, and that beasts partake of rational spirit. I'll admit" — I shrugged — "I sometimes have my doubts about certain kinds of Thomist. I mean, I've known a few who, if they have souls, keep them well hidden. But that's the exception that proves the rule."

His features relaxed. "I'm sorry. A silly question, really. Mind you, these days you have philosophers out there who deny that anyone at all — canine, anthropine, or lower on the scale of nature — has rational conscious-ness. We're all just organic machines to them. And as for extraordinary acts of consciousness, like those elephants…

well, they just deny they ever occur. And this means they have to pretend that vast regions of universally attested experience are just delusions and fabrications."

"Such as?"

"You know — fatidic dreams, knowledge of remote events, that sort of thing."

"Oh," I said uncertainly, "you mean the paranormal?"

Roland winced slightly. "I don't care for that word. But, well… I mean, ordinary consciousness isn't really reducible to purely physical causes, of course, but you know how these materialist savages, with all their abominable superstitions, can convince themselves it is. But what if there really are phenomena of mind that defy mechanistic paradigms completely? That violate locality, separability, causal contiguity…? I mean, well, look: have you ever dreamed something before it happened in precise detail, something you could not have predicted?"

"Yes," I said.

"And known others who had the same experience?"

"Yes. My father had some very vivid dreams like that."

Roland sighed and momentarily turned his eyes back to the moonlight beyond the window. "I miss your father. He was so kind."

Words would not come, so I simply nodded my head.

Roland looked at me again. "Have you ever suddenly known of something happening far away, something that you also could not have predicted?"

"On three occasions, definitely," I said. "All three were dreadful."

"Well, there you have it," said Roland. "I could go on too. But the point is, haven't most of us had those experiences? Or at least known others who have — other people we trust? Aren't there enough examples of these moments when the walls of material nature become like transparent glass — when a peregrine breeze momentarily lifts the veil aside and grants us a glimpse of what we shouldn't be able to see if we were just biochemical machines — to qualify as established data? To merit investigation? Or just curiosity?"

"Oh, you know," I said, "there's so-called 'paranormal' research, but I doubt it's very fruitful. If nothing else, these things are so episodic, and the causal logic is impossible to make sense of…"

Roland yawned loudly and scratched his right ear with his hind paw. "Balderdash. Anyway, I'm not talking about laboratory research, really. I just mean that scientists and philosophers who want to make sense of consciousness aren't going to do the subject much justice if they simply rule out any evidence that doesn't fit into a machine picture of the mind. The problem isn't method, but metaphysics. Dogmatic materialism makes them look for only mechanical causes, and to pretend that these other events never occur. It's all just fanaticism…fundamentalism. But, again, even ordinary mental events should make them surrender their prejudices — intentionality is every bit as fabulous and uncanny as telepathy — but they can't. I don't understand it. Dogs aren't like that. We're not…." He paused and laughed quietly. "We're not dogmatic. Sorry about that. Your father, with his taste for horrid puns, would have liked that."

"Yes, I'm afraid so."

Roland closed his eyes and lifted his nose, as if drawing in the moonlight as a fragrance. Then he looked at me and smiled. "I really do miss your father."

"So do I," I said, as the dream faded or changed (I cannot recall which).

# 3

# Roland on Free Will

I N MY DREAM (if it was a dream), I was roused by a soft, suave, gauzily sonorous voice, hauntingly reminiscent of Laurence Harvey's. "Are you doing anything just now?" it said. I opened my eyes to see the face of my dog Roland bent close over my own. Even in the dim light before dawn I could see the intent, pensive expression in his deep brown eyes and in the alert quivering of his coal-black nose.

"Nothing in particular," I murmured after a moment.

He stared at me a moment longer, sighed gently, and turned to retreat farther down the bed; settling by my feet on his haunches, he yawned languidly and said, "I didn't think so."

A few more moments passed in silence. "Is there anything on your mind?" I asked at last.

He lowered his head, heaved a louder, more lugubrious sigh, and said, "Freud."

Another pause ensued, and it became clear he had no intention of elaborating unbidden upon this curt, plaintive syllable.

"Sigmund?"

He looked at me with a hint of impatience. "Well, I certainly don't mean Lucian," he said. "The reason I can't sleep, and probably the reason you can't either, is that I just can't grasp what it was that everyone saw in him. I mean, I know the Freudian superstition has been largely discredited since those heady days—his results were falsified, his psychotherapeutic sorcery doesn't work, and so on — but that doesn't change the fact of the extraordinary hold his model of human motives still has over people's imaginations, or the bibulous excitement his ideas once inspired. Why? Was it because all that blather about the unconscious flatters human beings that they're the deepest mysteries in creation? Or that the key to reality can be found in their gastric or genital functions, or locked away in some little tin box concealed in one of their dreams?"

"Well, I..." I began.

But he had already become too animated to notice me. "I mean, just consider that whole silly psychic triad of id, ego, and superego: What makes it so profound to observe that we find ourselves drawn by opposing motives — the appetites of organism, the dictates of conscience — the glandular and the spiritual — so what? That's as great a revelation as noting that you have both a snout and a tail with a body wedged in between." He paused to gnaw briefly at his left flank and then turned back to me. "Would you like to scratch my stomach?"

"Not just now," I said. "So this is keeping you awake, is it?"

"Naturally," he replied with a slightly perplexed shake of his head. "It's just that it's such an obvious conceit, the whole tripartite psyche thing. You just notice that the self comprises contrary impulses and intentions, desires and drives, and *voilà*, there it is for you, ready-made. I want to do this, I feel compelled to do that, and here I am in the middle, poor chap. A dreary dialectic, oscillating back and forth across a gap spanning roughly the distance between epigastrium and cerebellum. The hierarchical picture is so obvious, such an immense banality. And it's all bound up with such a tawdry notion of persons' deepest drives."

"Yes, I see what you...."

"Now," Roland continued, "if you want to talk about the tripartition of the soul, repair to Plato. There you have something that really seems to make sense to me. The portrait is psychologically true: the perennial tension between the animal ecstasies of the flesh, which bind one to unthinking material necessity, and the rational freedom of the spirit, which is always striving to subdue the brute. What's that line from Yeats about the soul? 'Fastened to a dying animal?' Can't recall. Anyway, there's something truly free there, which is never the creature of an unhappy childhood or a frustrated hunger—spirit, *nous*, *Geist*—something that can convert the countervailing tempests of physiological urges into the elations of reason set free. Well...this is something dogs understand very well."

He fell silent and stared at me expectantly. The air about us had begun to grow more lustrous in the pearl-hued light. After several moments, though, he sighed yet again, as if despairing of my capacities, then turned and leapt down to the floor. A moment later, however, his face reappeared over the foot of the bed and, after three more seconds, he leapt back up and seated himself again. "It's all about freedom, you see," he said; "that's what this whole late modern psychomachy is about. It's a passion for determinism, physiological or subconscious or socioeconomic or what have you. It's all to do with the final triumph of the mechanistic philosophy in every sphere, even that of consciousness. How silly. As if machines could delight in bacon, or in the *chasse sauvage* when some impudent rabbit

scampers past one's nose, or in that romp that amuses
you so — what's it called? 'Fetch?' But nothing so excites
the modern materialist as the possibility of proving that
consciousness is reducible to physiology, that freedom
is an illusion, that mind is a ghostly epiphenomenon
of unconscious metabolisms. Every aspiring young
materialist dreams of growing up to be a robot."

"I expect you're right," I said.

"Think of those experiments where a subject is
instructed to twitch a wrist or push a button whenever
he feels moved to do so, and then to report when he
consciously made the choice to do it. Then electrodes
on the scalp or an MRI can show that a neural impulse
precedes the conscious choice by anywhere from one
to ten seconds, and the researcher can predict when
the subject will perform the action about 70% of the
time. So the scientist concludes that the *real* decision
is just some autonomic electrical flicker in the brain,
while the conscious decision is just a posterior accretion.
One scientist, that Haynes fellow, even said this renders
the existence of free will an 'implausible' hypothesis."

"I've never heard of him."

"But it makes no sense," Roland continued, more
emphatically. "There's absolutely no logical connection
between that experiment and that conclusion. It's an
eisegetical *non sequitur*. It just shows that a scientist's
interests frequently dictate what he thinks he's observed.
He goes looking for a mechanical transaction, so he
artificially extracts his data from their actual context,
and then miraculously discovers what he has predes-
tined his experiment to disclose. The far more sensible
conclusion would have been just the opposite: that
these results confirm the *reality* of rational freedom.

My only hesitancy is that, if the subject were absolutely free, one should be able to predict his actions in that situation with 100% accuracy."

I did not want to admit that I was not following his argument, but after several seconds had to: "Why, exactly?"

Roland gazed at me tenderly and shook his head. "Because the subject did exactly what he had freely undertaken to do. He was asked, of his own volition, to act whenever he felt the impulse to do so, and that's what he did. He wouldn't have been twitching a wrist or pushing a button otherwise. But the researchers work by the bizarre fiction that they are witnessing an isolated mechanical process without any prior premise, rather than a premeditated act prosecuted intentionally, so they produce the monstrous fantasy that they have proved that the whole act is reducible to a spontaneous physical urge. I mean, the experiment they imagine they've run isn't even logically possible, because there's no visible intentional content in any given electrical impulse that identifies it with any particular act. You have to know what is freely intended beforehand in order to know what the original neural event might portend. You have to know that the subject chose *in advance* to translate the impulse into an action. The urge doesn't go directly to its goal without crossing the interval of consciousness. So what's the point? That we often feel an urge before we freely decide whether to act on it? Well, you don't need electrodes on the scalp to prove that. But the urge is never isolated, because at both ends there's a decision of the conscious mind: undertaking to act in accord with a prompting, then choosing to submit to that prompting. In between there's some raw physiological agitation, which those free intentions have shaped into an accomplished deed. Let's just say that that's the material substrate, and that the intellect that makes the choices is a kind of formal cause: It's always shaping impulse into intentional action — prospectively, retrospectively...synoptically."

"Yes, all right," I said.

"I mean, there's always some prior and final act of the mind, some more capacious realm of intention for any impulse that's embodied and enacted. Yes? So you can't ever arrive at a deeper foundation. The researcher can never retreat to a more original moment, some discrete instant when a physical urge exists wholly outside that free movement of the mind. That object just isn't found in nature. Just you try to find it and you'll see."

"No, I believe you," I said.

But then, as the morning light was becoming positively silver, and as Roland began thoughtfully licking his left shoulder, I fell asleep again, or dreamed I had.

# 4

# Roland on Vaikuṇṭha

AT FIRST THERE was only the vigorous snuf-
fling sound of an inquisitive snout near my brow,
then the sensation of humid breath falling tenderly upon my neck, then the light brush of a cool wet
nose against my cheek, and finally the tentative probing
tip of a broad ductile tongue along the rim of my ear. I
stirred, an inarticulate but vaguely interrogative moan
rising in my throat. At once, a voice hauntingly like
Laurence Harvey's said, "Yes, I thought you were awake."

I opened my eyes, and could tell from the deep, almost cerulean darkness that it was still night. A moment later I realized that the shape looming over me, silhouetted against the moon-drenched linen curtains of my window, was that of my dog Roland's shoulders and head. "What…?" I began.

"I can guess why you're so restless," he said. "I expect it's all the turmoil and vexation that all these debates you get involved in cause you. You really need to stop engaging in debate with this poor benighted Thomist fellow especially. You simply mustn't allow indignation or personal passion rob you of sleep."

"But I *was*…"

"And I know that some of it's because of your feelings for me…the arguments about animal consciousness, and animal rationality, and animal eschatology, and such…and, well…"—I could see his head drop slightly, almost shyly—"I'm genuinely moved." Then his silhouette lurched toward me and the edge of his tongue ran along the bridge of my nose. "That's the customary gesture," he helpfully explained as he moved back away, turning his head to one side so that the wan moonlight now framed his glistening nose in a jeweler's foil of pale silver.

I thought it best to say nothing.

"Though I can see the temptation," he continued. "I see that in his latest posting he does concede the biblical imagery of cosmic redemption, but then goes on to say that this doesn't mean that one should take the eschatological imagery of animals and such—Isaiah 11 and whatnot—literally, because along with all those straminivorous lions, and graminivorous bears, and erstwhile predators napping innocuously with their quondam prey there's also a little child shepherd, and there are nurslings and weaned infants sporting with adders and asps, and yet *Jesus* — and this is his dialectical *coup de grâce* — says people will live like angels in the age to come, unmarried, so where would those children be coming from?"

I groaned, involuntarily but as tolerantly as I could manage. "Yes, that's pretty ghastly," I murmured. "That's what happens when people trained in analytic theology perpetrate exegesis of biblical texts, I suppose. And Thomists — good God, traditionalist manualist Thomism is an emotional pathology, not a philosophy." I cleared my throat and rubbed my eyes, now resigned to remaining awake. "Of course," I added, yawning, "he'd be terrifically shocked by some of the more exotic specimens of antique Jewish and Christian angelology. And, you know, there's Gregory of Nyssa's mysterious reference to an angelic mode of reproduction, which may be more than just a *façon de parler*..."

"Yes, yes," interrupted Roland, "all very recherché. But his real argument is that *all* one has to conclude from scripture is that, as he puts it, '*something of*' the natural cosmos will enter into eternity, and for that the resurrected human body suffices — just a body without a world..." Here Roland laughed (at least, I think he did, though the sound he produced was indistinguishable from the noise he makes when regurgitating his morning "viridescent purgative" of grass), and then resumed with a hapless sigh: "So all that scriptural business about the 'restoration of all things,' and creation's glorification and deliverance from decay, the final hierarchical reordering of all creation under Christ, all the creatures of sky and land and sea rejoicing in a new creation...all of that means, basically, the annihilation of everything organic except for the exemplary distillate of residual human organs." A flash of nitid fangs told me he was grinning in wicked mirth. "You know how it is: sometimes you have to destroy the universe to save it."

"Yes," I said after a moment, "it's pretty confused."

"I have to say, though, I think you tend to take the positions you do chiefly because you're a Hindu."

"I'm sorry," I said, all at once bewildered: "Because I'm a *Hindu*?"

"Precisely," said Roland. "So you're naturally going to see things from a different angle."

"But, I'm not…"

"You naturally think of all living things in terms of the *jiva* within, which is a spiritual reality more original than — transcendent of — species."

"But…"

"The poor karmic vagabond," Roland continued, morosely shaking his head, "the wanderer between lives: now a cow, now a man, now a god, now a paramecium…"

"Look," I interrupted, forcibly enough at last to break in upon his thoughts, "there's some misunderstanding here. I'm not Hindu."

Here again, I believe, Roland laughed. Then with a hapless sigh he said, "Really? Then why do you have all those volumes of Sanskrit and all those Indian books and…"

"Asian religions and literatures are one of my passions," I said, "one of my fields of study. But that's not the same…"

"Yes, yes," he said. "Anyway, the next piece you write should…"

"Look," I protested, "I'm tired. You write something."

At once, a cold silence descended, and lingered several moments. When Roland spoke again, his voice had dropped in register, sounding now like Stewart Granger's: "You know very well they wouldn't print it. We've talked about that particular glass ceiling before."

"Oh, nonsense…"

"So what you need to do now," he continued, "is raise the deeper question: not, say, 'Can animals be saved?' but 'Can persons be?'"

I briefly tried to deduce (or at least intuit) his meaning, conscious of having given him the impression in the past of a certain sluggishness of wits on my part; but I soon gave up. "You'd better explain."

"Well, all religious pictures of the last things are little more than dream images, shadows moving on the other side of veils of hope and horror. Whenever people try to foresee a state of things beyond time, whether they're Christians, Jews, Sikhs, Hindus like you…"

"I'm telling you…"

"…and imagine themselves participating in the reality they summon up from the fancies and longings in their souls, and from the metaphors and myths of their religious traditions, the issue is what it is they think can be saved *in themselves* and *in others*. It's a moral question, isn't it? It's a question of the metaphysics of persons."

"I…suppose so…"

"Persons, that is, as opposed to anonymous essences. I mean, look, you know how Peter Lombard and Aquinas said the sight of the sufferings of the damned will increase the beatitude of the redeemed, as pity would darken the joy of heaven?"

"Hard to forget," I said.

"And you know how many thinkers in the past have tried to make sense of the idea of heaven and hell as an eternal division breaking right through the middle of families, of friendships, of loyalties and allegiances and loves? How they've all had to presume that the sufferings of the damned will either be clouded from the eyes of the blessed or, worse, increase the pitiless delights of heaven?"

"Yes," I said with a grimace.

"And then there's this odd American philosopher who suggests God might keep the saved happy by deleting their damned loved ones from their memories."

I winced.

"But what's a person?" Roland suddenly barked. "What's a personal identity except a whole history of associations, loves, memories, attachments…? If those are removed, if one's loves are lost or converted into indifference, or even into satisfaction at the torment of those once loved…or even just forgetfulness…even just the forgetfulness of, well, *pets*—distasteful word—what is it that's saved? Surely someone else—something else—altogether: a spiritual anonymity…a vapid spark of pure intellection…the residue of a soul that's been… reduced to no one."

I merely shrugged.

"Have you read any Michel de Certeau?" he asked.

"Yes," I said, surprised, "of course. I didn't know you had."

"Oh yes," he said, as if I were foolish to doubt it, "he has quite a following in canine philosophical circles. Especially among spaniels, because of their special tradition of 'oblique exegesis,' or '*interpretatio obliqua*.' But I mention him just because of that lovely line of his…

what is it? 'The I is the place of another?' Something
like that. Well, anyway, there's the point: as a person,
as a living actuality in communion with a world and
with others, my spiritual identity is constituted by all
my encounters, my memories, my affinities, intimate
or remote. I *am* others. And so how could I truly *be*
in heaven when those I love are in hell? Wouldn't I in
some sense—the person I am—be in hell with them?
As Abraham Lincoln said about heaven, it's everyone
or no one. That's not merely a warm sentiment; it's an
irrefutable logical maxim."

"Lincoln?"

"The old argument, I suppose," he said: "the imper-
sonalist Advaita Vedānta of Śaṅkara over against the
personalist Viśiṣṭādvaita of Rāmānuja."

"I suppose so," I said, beginning to feel weary.

"But neither school really thinks of persons as persons, probably, in quite the way Westerners do—in
quite the particular, contingent…fragile way, that is."

"I suppose not," I replied, feeling still wearier.

Roland became quiet momentarily, then stretched
out and lay down, pressing up against my side. "You
love the *Mahābhārata*, don't you?" he said.

I was momentarily taken aback. "Yes," I said; "I love
few books better."

"And Karṇa is your favorite character?"

"Yes. Why?"

"Well," he said with a yawn, "Karṇa's not the point.
It's just that all this makes me think of that last lovely
tale in the *Svargarohana Parva* where, decades after
the battle of Kurukṣetra, and well after the death of
Kṛṣṇa, the five Pāṇḍavas and their beloved Draupadī
leave their kingdom, depart from Indraprastha, and

try to ascend to Svarga, Indra's heaven, in the flesh. But as they climb the Himalayas they fall, one by one, into crevasses or down cliff faces: beautiful Draupadī, clever Sahadeva, winsome Nakula, invincible Arjuna, mighty Bhīma…till only Yudhiṣṭhira, great king of righteousness, remains. He alone reaches the gates of Amrāvatī, the blissful gardens of Svarga, and the gods welcome him; but, at the last moment, they say he can't bring with him a dog who's loyally followed him all the way from Indraprastha, as dogs are animals of ill omen, fond of crematory grounds and with unfastidious eating habits." Roland sighed deeply. "I suppose my fondness for Sevruga caviar wouldn't get me in. But, anyway, wonderfully, for that dog's sake, Yudhiṣṭhira refuses to enter paradise. 'He did not abandon me; I'll not abandon him.' Greyfriar's Bobby at the pearly gates…"

"Yes," I said, "but then of course the dog turns out to be Yama, god of dharma, testing Yudhiṣṭhira's virtue one last time."

"Right," said Roland with another sigh. "A distinctly unsatisfactory narrative trick. The tale *seems* subversive at first, and allows for another demonstration of Yudhiṣṭhira's goodness, but then doesn't *really* break the rules governing that restricted neighborhood. Oh well. Not the last time a dramatic impasse would be resolved by an implausible *deus ex canili*."

"Perhaps he'd have been better off if the dog had really been just a dog," I said.

"I know: because he finds the Kauravas in Svarga, in bliss," said Roland, "but finds his brothers and wife in torment down in the darkness of Naraka, atoning for unpurged lapses of dharma."

"Yes," I said. "Though that's only for a season. In the

end, they'll reach paradise and be reconciled with the Kauravas. And Yudhiṣṭhira himself ascends beyond Svarga, to the Vaikuṇṭha of Viṣṇu, the very heaven of God, never to be reborn. And, of course, dogs can attain *jīvanmukti* also..."

"But not as dogs," said Roland in a dour whisper; "only after many 'higher' rebirths..."

"The purblindness and prejudices of all religious traditions," I said softly. "They mean well."

Roland was silent for nearly a minute. Then, quietly, hesitantly, he said, "Would you do it for me? Forsake Indra's paradise, I mean?"

"Without a second thought."

"Truly?"

"Of course," I said, closing my eyes. "Dogs are better than gods."

"Well, that goes without saying," Roland replied.

And then I was asleep.

# 5

# Roland on Dreams

I T WAS, I believe, the third time the small, hard, moist rubber ball struck my forehead and dropped to my pillow that I awakened fully (or dreamed I had done). The gaze that met my own was that of my dog Roland, his coal-black snout, drooping brown ears, and handsome chalk-and-charcoal face so beautifully illuminated by the pale golden glow of the rushlight beyond my open bedroom door that he looked like a saint or *bodhisattva* wrapped in a haze of glory.

"Ah," I said, clearing my throat and slightly raising my head, "yes… I don't actually have any treats with me just now, and…"

But he interrupted me with his soft, slightly amused voice (so hauntingly reminiscent of Laurence Harvey's): "No, no, I'm not playing that silly 'Give' game you like so much."

"Oh," I said, still gathering my wits. "Then why…?"

"I was wondering whether you were dreaming," said Roland; "and, if so, whether you'd be able to recognize the transition from one state to the other if I roused you." His snout momentarily came nearer and he briefly sniffed about my lips and nostrils. "Yes," he said, drawing back again, "you seem alert now. So—can you?"

I cleared my throat again. "Well, yes…of course."

"Are you sure?" said Roland, drawing out the last syllable doubtfully. "Can you really?"—again, the last word skeptically prolonged.

"Of course," I answered. "Why do you even ask?"

He sighed, smiled morosely, rose and moved several feet down the length of the bed, then turned and sat, facing me again. "I can't help but notice that when you write about our conversations you usually describe them as occurring in dreams."

"Yes," I murmured, trying to focus my mind on some thought or memory that seemed to have slipped just out of sight. "That seems...right.... I mean, they do all occur late at night, and to follow from some dream or other...and..."

"Dear me," chortled Roland, gently shaking his head, "there's a venerable logical error for you: *post somnium ergo propter somnium*; sequence proves consequence; the cockerel heralds the dawn, hence its song must have conjured the sun. Really...and you with pretensions to philosophy."

"Yes," I said uncomfortably, feeling something of the force of his rebuke. "But they do seem, at least in retrospect..."

"*Seem*?" he growled playfully. "And here I'd hoped you'd be able to judge precisely from the phenomenal feelings of the situation...its distinctive *qualia*." He lowered his head pensively and, after a few moments, added, "Of course, I suppose that begs the principle. What really distinguishes a dream from wakefulness, after all? If experience is just the phenomenal translation of some occultly noumenal *res ignota*, where can we really locate the boundary...the point of quantitative intensity within the qualitative continuum that marks the division between what we call dream and what we call reality? In a sense, the whole world is the dream of the representing intellect." He paused, gazed at me for a moment, and then sniffed tentatively at my shin; then he sighed again.

"What?" I asked after another moment.

"Just trying to discern your mood."

"From my scent?"

Roland's brow furrowed and a look of pained disappointment appeared on his face. "Of course. How else? There's a reason why the olfactory is called the most divine of the senses."

"I believe that's actually said about vision."

At once the look of disappointment dissolved into an expression of affectionate mirth, and Roland shook his head wonderingly. "Primates are so adorable. What nonsense. What sense is feebler and more fallible? The eyes take in only surface impressions, and are so easily deceived by masks or shrouds or peculiarities of perspective or optical illusions. They're no use at all in the darkness. They're the fools of every false smile, every feigned laugh that conceals a stiletto. But the nose—ah, that pierces every veil of dissimulation, penetrates the night as easily as the day, faithfully guides one through Stygian darkness or winding labyrinths, finds out the truth the liar involuntarily betrays, the hidden intent, the secret fear—a man can control his lips, but not his pheromones—and is never prey to false appearances. *In naribus veritas*, as the ancient wisdom has it. It's the only sense that goes right to the core of the self. It's the very window of the soul. *Nasus ad nasum loquitur*. Antony forsook all the glory and power of Rome not for Cleopatra's eyes, but for her nose. No, no—olfaction is, as I say, the most godlike of the senses."

"Yes," I began, "all right, I…"

"I mean," Roland continued, "if you were, say, hiding some bacon about your person, and I were forced to rely on my poor, pitiable, credulous eyes to discover it, I'd..." But then he paused, glanced at me suspiciously, lifted his snout and sniffed hopefully about, and then sighed yet again. "Well, I'd have no chance. Vision is nothing but a dream within a dream.... Maybe that's why it's so hard for you, come to think of it. How hard it must be for an ophthalmocentric ape to distinguish reality from fantasy."

"Well, I don't think it's any harder..."

"That reminds me," Roland said, yawning magnificently, "I've a question that you might be best able to answer, being a Hindu."

"Oh, that again," I said, unable to suppress an exasperated groan. "Look, I'm not..."

"Yes, yes," he said with an indulgent grin. "None of your games. Just tell me how you'd translate 'māyā' from the Sanskrit."

"Oh," I said, trying to raise the angle of my pillow slightly, "well, it comes from the same Indo-European word as *mageia*, *magia* — magic — and means something like the power of creation, power to produce... especially God's infinite power to create."

"And yet," said Roland, "most of us in the West assume it simply means 'illusion.' Why is that?"

"Yes, well, in a certain school of Vedānta, and then elsewhere, that became its special acceptation. Ādi Śaṅkara certainly used it, not to indicate that the world is unreal, but that our false understanding or ignorance — our *avidyā* — makes us perceive reality as separate from God..."

"*Avidyā!*" It was an almost triumphant bark. "That's

what I mean. Your Indo-European roots are showing. 'Not seeing,' 'failing to *see*.' Reliance on the eyes cuts you off from God."

"Now, wait…"

"I'm joking," said Roland with a gentle snort. "All the senses dream, I know…or, rather, all dreams have phenomenal forms. Ghostly music, phantom palaces, fragrances from the banquets of the gods…the honey of a lover's lips…the prick of a thorn. I suppose that's why primate culture is so uncertain of what dreams are: whether Thomas Browne is right — '*visions, and phantasticall objects wherin wee are confessedly deceaved… fictions and falsehoods…*' — or whether they're visitations from beyond the Gates of Horn, truths written in the symbolic language of gods and angels, which only oneiromancy or oneirocriticism can elucidate to the waking mind…if there is such a thing as the waking mind." He licked his shoulder pensively, then sniffed my shin again. "*Cognitio vespertina*, evening knowledge — isn't that the scholastic term for the synthetic knowledge of finite intellects? *Cognitio somnians* might be better. Did Chuang-Tzu dream he was a butterfly, or was he a butterfly dreaming himself to be Chuang-Tzu? What's the *ontological* difference between the phantasmic or represented empirical world within all of us and the noonday reveries of some ectothermic animal, like a lizard or a Californian, drowsing in the sun? Really, you Hindus, at least the Vaiṣṇavas, might have the best image there is of creation's ground: Viṣṇu fast asleep, in bliss, embowered in the loving coils of Ananta Śeṣa, afloat on the Sea of Milk, hearing the sweet lullabies pouring from the great nāga's mouths, dreaming all things into being…and, asleep in each of us, that same divine awareness…so that we're nearest God in dreaming within his dream…" Roland raised his eyes now and gazed directly into mine. "Novalis knew—knew what we long for in finding God: that 'last morning…when the light does not scare the night and love away… *wenn der Schlummer ewig und nur ein unerschöpflicher Traum sein wird'*—when that sleep within becomes 'eternal…just an inexhaustible dream.' Maybe the Oceanian aborigines saw it all long ago. Everything comes from the Dreaming…the time before time, the place beyond time…and we dream the world within the greater Dreaming…"

"I think that might be a mistranslation, actually," I ventured, hoping to curtail the rhapsody before it became a symphony.

But Roland took no notice. He merely stretched his forepaws out before him, lay down fully against my legs, and continued speaking, half to me and half to himself: "And we come from there and go to there… and perhaps choose the time of our coming hither and our going hence…and perhaps not. But still…we come from the Dreaming and to the Dreaming we return… all is the Dreaming…"

But here, I believe, I was asleep again.

6

# Roland on the Secret Soul

I WAS, IT SEEMED, standing in my garden, gazing through shifting silvery curtains of mist at the muted yellow of a flowering forsythia. Somehow I knew it was only a little past dawn. I might have gone inside after a moment had I not heard the garden gate behind me swinging on its steel hinges and then the soft click of its latch. When I turned to look, I could see nothing through the haze; but after a moment a small figure appeared, at first like a wavering phantom, then assuming the solid, mottled, familiar form of my dog Roland. Dangling from his mouth by a thick silken cord was what after some seconds I recognized as a Japanese *koto*, though one of unusually small design. On seeing me, he started back slightly, furrowed his brow, then strolled over to the low wooden deck of the house and gently set the instrument down. Returning, he stared at me thoughtfully and said (in a voice curiously similar to Laurence Harvey's), "You never rise this early. Is all well?"

"Yes," I said, in an unexpectedly hoarse voice, "I think so. I don't recall…"

But now Roland was energetically sniffing at my left hand.

"Honestly," I said, "nothing's wrong."

He sighed, gazed intently upward into my eyes for a long uncertain moment, and then said, "Very well." Then he began to turn away.

"Wait," I said. "Where have you been, with…that?" I pointed at the *koto*.

Roland smiled and sat down upon his haunches. "I was afraid you'd ask." He shrugged. "It's something I occasionally do. I spent the night in the hall of the local *daimyo* performing passages from the *Heike Monogatari*…the battle of Dan-no-ura…and…" — he lowered his eyes somewhat bashfully — "declaiming some of my own verse."

"There's a local *daimyo*?" I began.

He raised his snout, his head at a quizzical tilt. "Of course. Who do you think makes sure the local peasantry plants enough glutinous rice for wine…or protects them from the depredations of the *yakuza*?"

"Your verse?" My drowsy wits had only just caught up to his words. "You write poetry?"

Again he looked away, almost shyly, another faint smile on his lips. "I keep that side of my life quiet. Actually, last night was a celebration of my most recent volume of haiku."

"Most recent?"

"Just a hundred poems, one to a page, each with an English gloss at the foot."

"You wrote them in Japanese?"

Roland met my eyes again, now with his customary expression of longanimous affection. "Of course. It's not a form that suits other tongues."

"What are they, um, about?" I asked feebly.

"Transience," he replied mildly. "The evanescent moment, the fading day, the ephemeral blossom. I try merely to capture the delicate essence of a passing moment—its tone, its texture, its exquisite impermanence—and something of that anguished yearning for eternity that's expressible, mysteriously enough, only in images of transitoriness." He sighed deeply and shook his head. "Who knows if I succeed? How can any artist share more than a distant, dying echo of his inspirations?" He paused for a moment, met my eyes searchingly, and then—almost shyly—dropped his gaze again. "I could recite one for you…if you'd like. There's one perfect for this setting."

A thrill of sentiment passed through me; I felt genuinely touched. "Yes, please," I said, "if you would."

He smiled that gentle smile once more, straightened his back, stared away into the pearl-hued emptiness, and spoke in a clear, measured voice:

"Cool mists at morning,
Trembling leaves gleam with dew — *Ah!* —
An earthworm's fragrance."

He fell silent, continued gazing away for several moments, then bowed his head meditatively. "Well?" he asked.

"Yes," I replied, a bit uncomfortably, "I see what you mean about…it suiting the scene."

After a moment Roland raised his head and, with a suspicious scowl, asked, "Nothing else?"

"I don't know," I replied. "I mean, for me that last line…isn't so evocative."

"Don't be absurd," he said with a curt laugh. "It's the piquant master-stroke. What captures the feel of the morning more than the fragrance of earthworms — that strange, sharp, vinegar-and-musk pungency, those hints of clay and minerals, that faint soupçon of scorched saltiness…?"

"You see, I don't have your nose."

Roland shrugged wearily. "No, I suppose not. Describing a sunset to someone blind from birth." He sighed again. "The translation detracts from the effect as well."

"I imagine," I said.

"But that's a perennial problem — mediating between tongues, cultures, sensibilities…souls. Certainly all my translation work often feels like trying to change iron into satin, or butter into wine."

"Do you do much translating?"

"I'm divulging all my little secrets today," he said with a snort. Then he sniffed at the grass at his feet, bit off a few blades, chewed slowly, and swallowed. "In my small way, yes. I'm working on certain unjustly

neglected epics: the *Punica* of Silius Italicus and the
*Dionysiaca* of Nonnus. Though in the former case the
neglect is more understandable: the enormous length...
and some of the same aesthetic oddity as Camões, with
that uneven mix of historical and mythical materials.
Nonnus is more important. I mean, where would the
best poets of late antiquity have been without him —
Dracontius, Musaeus, Colluthus — or the Byzantines —
Planudes, Genesius? But how to render his language
into another tongue? It's so rich, diverse, gorgeously
involved and imbricated — he was the greatest virtu-
oso of *poikilia* — and his... well, his gongorism is more
perversely complicated than the most bombastic Alex-
andrian grammarian's allegory on the alphabet... or
whatever. How to capture that wild polyphony?" He
shook his head, perhaps a little morosely. "That's why
there's no good translation of Virgil — so much is in
the pure music of the verse."

"True."

"But the problem's deeper than that," he continued.
"If translation were just a system of mechanical corre-
spondences, one sign for another, for which one could
devise non-semeiotic algorithms... But, no, it's about
meanings, and it's all dependent on spiritual tact — or
spiritual senses, really, able to perceive implications,
atmospheres, nuances... not only what an author
expresses, but also what he doesn't need to express.
One renders the words, but one *translates* the text as the
product of an intentionality, with a purposive dimension that one has to share in to understand the work
at all. That's why there'll never be a computer program
for real translation. One has to know the whole before
understanding the parts, and more than the whole

before understanding the whole. One has to intend the author's intention, and that means in part retreating to a level of consciousness prior to individual identity."

"I'm not sure…"

But Roland was too preoccupied with his own thoughts to notice me. "We've talked before about the irreducibility of intentional consciousness to material forces — its teleological orientation toward a transcendental horizon beyond nature and its origination in a pure awareness prior to empirical identity — and about how the whole world of nature is constituted only in the relation between these two poles outside of physical nature…"

"I believe…"

"That's where the real work of translation is done: that original pure act of consciousness, more inward than our inmost, higher than our utmost, to which the mystics ascend by going inward…oh, you know, Eckhart's *Seelesburg*, in whose heart dwells the *Fünklein Gottes*. Or the ātman that is more original than the *jīva* in its individuality. Do you know the Sufi idea of the seven layers of the soul?"

"Yes, I do. I…"

"The more one descends into the *nafs*, the higher one rises, the nearer to the hidden garden, till one reaches the secret soul, the *ruh sirr*, which remembers God, and beyond that — more inward yet — one draws near to the secret of secrets, the *sirr-ul-asrar*, where the divine spark shines. Or think of Teresa of Ávila's interior castle, with its seven chambers, and the divine throne at the center… Well, it's somewhere in those inner realms that translation occurs because, the more deeply one enters in, the more expansive one becomes, the more the veils of our small exclusive empirical egos fall away before the naked light of that original and ultimate truth. That's also where all art is born, violating the boundary between the calculating mind and that purer dimension of consciousness, where one finds the transcendent ground and end of mind not as a concept, but almost as an immediate intuition. That's why the true artist is to the philosopher as an angel to a worm…and why a true translator is someone who drinks from that same spring."

Roland fell silent. I stared at him for several seconds through the slowly drifting mists, and then said, "You're a very unusual dog."

He raised his eyes and looked at me with an expression somewhere between disappointment and indulgent fondness. "You know," he said, "remarks of that sort are well-intended, but they also reveal some unreflective and distasteful prejudices." He sighed yet again. Then he rose, bestowed a mollifying lick upon my hand, trotted over to the deck, retrieved his *koto*, and continued on toward the back door of the house.

PART TWO

# THE FINAL
# SEVEN COLUMNS

# 1

# Roland on Causality

I HAD LAIN DOWN on the daybed in my home office with, I seem to recall, a headache, not long after dinner and intending to get up again within the hour. Instead, it seems, I had fallen fast asleep. On opening my eyes, I was immediately aware that the night was now well advanced. The gelid light of the moon—which was near to reaching its apogee—was streaming into the room through the eastward facing window over the bed, and for a few seconds I simply stared into it, somewhat annoyed to realize I had let the evening slip away without completing any of the small, irksome, but necessary tasks I had intended to discharge before retiring. Then, however, I realized that, even though no lamp was lit, it was not only the moon that was illuminating the room. I turned to look at my computer and saw that it was turned on and radiating its familiar bleak nimbus of ghastly fluorescence. I also saw why: there, seated in my office chair in one-quarter profile, staring into the screen with one paw resting on the mouse, was my dog Roland. Despite the angle, I was able to see his face fully, because it was mirrored on the screen before him in the open photograph program he was using to take pictures of himself. This was odd enough, since Roland is anything but a vain dog—though one could easily understand it if he were, what with his striking shorthaired coat of mottled white, brown, and black fur, and with that coal-black nose of his, and those deep brown eyes, and that arrestingly handsome face. But the scene was rendered all the more bizarre by two additional features: the first was a summer fedora of dark tan straw with a gray headband, which was perched on his head at a distinctly cocky tilt; the second was the expression of wild, positively histrionic happiness he was wearing on his face—his eyes wide, his head turned ever so invitingly to one side, his lips open and pulled back into an extravagant grin, his tongue extended in apparently irrepressible canine mirth—as though he were imitating the slipcover of one of Sinatra's "*Veni Mecum*" albums for Capitol, but attempting to exude even more vulgar charm. It was all so out of keeping with his typically restrained and dignified comportment that I could not contain myself.

"What in God's name are you doing?" I croaked, and then cleared my throat. "You look like you're practicing for a cabaret act."

His exuberant grin immediately resolved into a slight, merely bemused, perhaps mildly sardonic smile. He removed his paw from the mouse and pushed away from the desk so that the chair swiveled around toward me. "*Der Schläfer erwacht*," he said quietly, in a voice that reminded me of Laurence Harvey uttering one of his bitterer lines in *Butterfield 8*. "Don't you approve of the hat?"

"Oh, that," I replied, slowly swinging my legs over the edge of the bed and sitting upright, "*that's* very dashing. It suits you. I was referring to the antic facial expressions you were affecting."

He pursed his lips. "A little too…*meretricious* perhaps?"

"Well, I don't know if I'd…" I momentarily gritted my teeth. "Actually, *yes*, since you ask—for you, at least. Maybe not for the MC at a beauty pageant, but definitely for you."

He sighed. "Well, it's your fault, you know."

I stretched my arms and then rubbed my forehead. "How so?" I asked.

"It's that book you wrote about me," he said, shaking his head slightly. "You seem to have made me famous… in a small way, at least. Ever since it appeared, I've received a constant flow of fan mail, increasing in volume and frequency month by month, and I simply can't answer it all, despite being as punctilious by nature as you know I am. So I thought I would take a photograph of the sort that celebrities send out to their adoring votaries, print up several copies with a virtual autograph, and send them out to my fans accompanied by a standardized note of thanks. It seemed the easiest way to deal with their queries and entreaties and… occasional embarrassingly candid confessions."

"Confessions?"

"Well, if you *will* portray me as some kind of a sage, you mustn't be surprised if a few of your more impressionable readers conclude that I can provide them spiritual guidance."

"I see," I said. For a moment I looked away to the window, coldly ablaze with lunar splendor. "A full moon tonight, I believe," I murmured. I turned my eyes back to Roland. "I didn't portray you as anyone except who you are, you know. That book was almost painfully honest from beginning to end. My fidelity to the facts…"

"Was exemplary, I know," he interrupted in a conciliatory tone. "It's not really your fault. I was being facetious. Neither of us foresaw the consequences. And I imagine that in time the flood of correspondence will become a trickle and then drain away altogether. At the moment, however, this is all I can think to do to avoid rudeness without enslaving myself to my own fame."

"I should have foreseen it," I said. "That's why one should avoid disclosing too much of one's private life to the public. It was inevitable."

Roland smiled more indulgently now. "A causal determinist forsooth," he said. "You couldn't have known. There was a whole constellation of contributing causes — unanticipated contingencies, adventitious agencies, chance circumstances — that you couldn't have predicted." Here, however, he wrinkled his brow, and for a moment he seemed to be distracted by some new thought that was just now occurring to him. "Then again…" he began, but then fell silent.

"What?" I asked after a few seconds.

He turned his eyes to me as if now only half aware of my presence. "I wonder if that's really the right way to think of it." Then he shook his head, clearly waking from his momentary revery, and emitted a small laugh. "Forgive me, but it's just struck me that maybe the issue is *how* we might have foreseen what would happen — I mean, by what means should one try to predict a future series of causes and effects? The empirical and statistical calculation of mechanical forces? Or the logical calculation of intrinsic relations between various rationales? Surely the latter if one is working within any context more complex than that of a billiards table or a collapsing star. The former only in instances of causality considered as isolated systems of energetic interaction."

I hesitated at first to ask him what he meant, knowing that he was probably waiting for me to do so, but I soon relented. "I'm not sure I follow you," I said.

The indulgent smile returned to his face, now with an additional element of pitying tenderness in it. "I mean, how do we conceive of causes, at all levels of agency? We all know Laplace's fantasy that a superlatively percipient demon fully apprised of the disposition of every particle in existence could reconstruct the entire history of the universe and predict its entire future; and we also all know that it's false, if only because of the thermodynamical naïveté that such a view depends upon, or because of its unrefined pre-quantum corpuscularism. But, even if one could theoretically correct for entropic indeterminacies or quantum non-locality or whatever else, it would still be incredible to me as a picture of reality. I simply do not know how anyone can believe that the universe is a fixed mechanical continuum determined wholly by exchanges of energy between material objects and forces. In fact, I regard that very way of thinking of causality as a physicalist myth, which experience exposes as a fiction in every moment and which even contemporary physics presumes only as a practical convenience, when Newtonian physical models produce sufficiently finely approximate calculations for one's purposes."

"This seems a rather abstruse way of thinking about fan letters..." I began.

"You know," Roland continued, apparently taking no note of me, "I was just re-reading Schopenhauer's *The Fourfold Root of the Principle of Sufficient Reason* yesterday and I found myself mentally stumbling over his reproaches of Aristotle—and of Aristotle's ancient and mediaeval intellectual kith — for not having adequately or consistently distinguished between causes and reasons. To Schopenhauer's mind, evidently, a cause was something that resulted in a change in physical state — or, rather, it was *nothing but* that change of causal state, as viewed from its prior condition rather than its posterior effect — and was marked by a consecutive order moving from past to future. Full stop. A reason, by contrast, is a logical entailment, a rationale, even perhaps an analytic truth, but not an instance of change or a modification of a physical state. And this distinction, in one form or another, is of course a fixed feature of most modern philosophical thought, taken almost without exception as an evident truth and a significant advance over the murkier causal metaphysics of pre-modern epochs. But is that right?" He looked at me inquiringly, as if expecting me to supply an answer.

"I suppose," I said after a moment, trying to seem deeply thoughtful, "the first question is how might it be wrong."

"True," said Roland, slowly nodding, "very true. I suspect that Schopenhauer and a great many modern philosophers have actually traded an ancient insight for a modern superstition and then deceived themselves that they've profited by the transaction. Maybe they're the ones who are the prisoners of unexamined prejudice, and of an unreflective and incomplete world-view. When Aristotle and other ancient Greek-speaking thinkers used the word '*aitia*' — or when Latin-speaking thinkers used '*causa*' — to indicate things modern thinkers would discriminate into the separate camps of causes and reasons, perhaps they were merely recognizing something today's philosophers have

forgotten, or to which they've been rendered insensible
by centuries of mechanistic thinking. Maybe they saw
and immediately understood that the only intelligible
concept of causation is one that encompasses an ana-
logical continuity between different kinds of logical—
*logical*—relation, and that even the physical exchange
of energy between objects in motion is a calculable
constant only because it is the emergent expression of
a deeper *rational* necessity."

"Ah," I said. "Well, 'Plato thought nature but a spume
that plays / Upon a ghostly paradigm of things...'"

"It's always back to Yeats with you."

I felt myself scowl in perplexity. "Is it? I don't think
I..."

"Anyway, what I mean is that it's a fundamental error
to imagine that the Aristotelian fourfold account of
causality is somehow a more primitive attempt at a
model of how physical forces interact with one another,
as if for him the 'origin of motion' and its '*telos*' and
'*hylē*' and 'form' were all species of efficiency, simulta-
neously and extrinsically exerting their powers on an
object or instance of physical change that they're determining from four different external trajectories—as if
an efficient causal force were pushing things forward
from outside while a final causal force were dragging
it forward also from outside, and form were a kind of
stamp impressing itself on a kind of ductile physical
medium called 'matter.' But that's wrong. Rather, these
*aitiai* are the field of rational relations in which anything and any event subsists as at once discrete and
yet part of the larger continuum of the cosmos. They
inhere *in* any reality, as what it is. They are an inseparable ensemble of logical coordinates, none of which

is intelligible in the absence of the others. And they're a grammar of predication. After all, if I wanted you to tell me what something is, what is it I'm seeking to know? Well, what its essential — its formal — characteristics are, and also perhaps what it's made of or how it subsists, and certainly how it came to be, and just as certainly what the full and therefore defining range of its potentials is. And, of course, these explanatory moments are not extrinsic to one another, but entirely implicit *in* one another. So it is that the *aitiai* of which ancient philosophy and science spoke were simply the logical and ontological coherence within whatever exists so long as it exists."

"But," I interrupted, "won't most modern philosophers and scientists simply say that any system of predicates is merely a way of describing an empirical reality, not the intrinsic constitution of that reality? Or…"

"But how could that be?" Roland asked, urgently enough that the question came out as a bark. "What sort of occasionalist magic would allow for the seeming harmony between the mechanical and noetic orders then? How could the mind know anything of a world that, of its nature, is not hospitable to or apparent in mind? I mean…" He took a deep breath. "The ancient picture of the world that's reflected in the Aristotelian system of *aitiai* is of a cosmos that's already mindlike in its frame and essence — already a noetic coherence — and as such is neither alien to nor independent of mind. The modern picture, which was in its origins only a methodological convention, was achieved precisely by exorcising mind and everything mindlike — form and finality that is, which is also to say substantial forms and intrinsic intentionality — from our picture of nature.

The new organon converted the cosmos into a mechanism so that it could be investigated inductively, in total abstraction from any purposive or ideal rationality. Not that it really could be, at least not past a certain elementary level. Any scientist engaged in examining a natural phenomenon must inevitably treat that phenomenon as an intentional process or design in order to understand it. It's then only a metaphysical dogma that dictates that the purposive deductive apparatus then be shelved as a mere instrumental fiction."

"True."

"And that's why it's impossible in the terms presumed by today's dominant naturalist metaphysics to re-integrate our experience of mind into our picture of nature."

"Also true."

"But then, as Hume demonstrated — and as Schopenhauer so well knew — causality, far from being explained, becomes instead inexplicable. Lacking any intrinsic rational structure, it's reduced to a mere black box, a mere series of phenomenal juxtapositions and associations, something science can measure in terms of variable quantities and exchanges of energy but certainly not elucidate in terms of necessary consequences. The principles embodied in those quantities and exchanges aren't transparent to those measurements. It may be merely a convention born of perception, for all we know, that makes us privilege the temporally antecedent over the consequent in assigning the designation of cause or effect to this or that aspect of this or that event of change. But that could be backwards for all we can tell by way of our bare quantifications. Maybe, even if nature really is a closed mechanical continuum, the real trajectory of causality is in essence 'attractive' rather than 'propulsive.' Maybe what we think of as the future actually exerts a determining causal force *toward* the present. All that can be observed and measured in the mechanical paradigm are contiguities, energetic expenditures and conservations, changes in state; but the sciences have no means by which to assign logical or even *causal* priority."

"Perhaps the smoke summons the fire?" I asked.

"Well, if nothing else, a transition in physical states is, in its own terms, simply a transition. After all, since in fact all causes and their effects are actually simultaneous, not successive, and given that in any interaction between, say, two physical forces or objects change goes both ways, and both forces or objects are modified by the interaction, what is it other than convention that dictates how we assign priority and posterity, or how we assign causal momentum? Simply said, mechanism doesn't explain. Rationales do."

Now I was the one who took a long deep breath. "Certainly I have no prejudice against form or teleology," I said. "But perhaps we're simply using the language of causality equivocally, and both uses are legitimate in their proper sphere."

Roland seemed to be pondering this for several seconds, staring away into the moonlight. But then he shook his head emphatically. "No," he said. "The mechanistic acceptation of the word 'cause' is simply too deficient in meaning and explanatory power to warrant that much semantic autonomy. Look, think, does it make sense to say that the regularities of physical causal phenomena explain the rational laws governing reality? Or is it rather the reverse that's the case: there is of necessity a rational order, a kind of syllogistic consistency to reality, that requires physical causality also to be consistent, and so predictable, and this alone, properly speaking, *explains* why it is so?"

I confess, it took me a few seconds to grasp what Roland was asking; but, when I did, I said, "The latter, I suppose."

"Quite so. Maybe, then, before causality is conceived as the brute mechanics of force, proceeding in unilinear fashion from past to future, it should be thought more deeply as the totality of a complete rational unity — like a mathematical equation, or a logically correct predicative sentence, in which subject, predicate, and copula are all properly entailed in one another. Or maybe the causal structure of the cosmos is rather like a musical score by a master composer, in which it's the finished totality that dictates the necessary structure of the music, the chord progressions, the thematic development, the contrapuntal architecture — even though it seems from the perspective of those listening to it when it's performed as if the final resolution of the whole composition is the *emergent* result of all those temporally prior forces...maybe a convergence of accidental lines of explication in a consonance produced by Darwinian algorithms of attrition and survival. I mean..." He paused and ran his tongue over his nose two or three times. "You surely recall when Thomas Nagel, who's certainly no theist, published his book arguing for the plausibility of a teleological conception of mind and cosmos, and then all those doctrinaire traditional materialists, like Richard Dawkins and Steven Pinker, made fools of themselves by attacking him as an Intelligent Design theorist."

I shrugged. "What else could they make of themselves?" I said. "You can't turn a sow's ear into a silk purse."

Roland rewarded me with an appreciative smirk. "Very good," he said. "*Touché*. Anyway, my point is that it was odd behavior on their part even from a materialist perspective. After all, surely they're perfectly *au fait* with the idea of multiple universes, and of universes being generated by fluctuations in a quantum foam, outside of spacetime. It would seem only a short step from there—given the way materialists think—to make the Darwinian argument that only certain kinds of universe can survive in that forbidding quantum landscape without collapsing immediately into themselves again, and those would be universes that exhibit the rational consistency of an equation...universes whose total sum, so to speak, as much determines the calculation as the reverse. Only such a universe would possess a *formal* consistency sufficient to survive the natural process of selection. Maybe all reality is in a sense organism, and all organism in a sense logic." Here he again turned his gaze to the moonlight and then fell silent for several moments, long enough for me to suspect that he had forgotten my presence altogether.

I cleared my throat and asked, "Are we still talking about your fan mail?"

He turned his gaze toward me, but his expression told me that his thoughts had not entirely returned from wherever they were wandering. "Isn't it curious how dogmatical materialists can be? They're so certain they *know* that the world is a closed, solely mechanical order, which the mind's power of representation

posteriorly translates into something mindlike, something conformable to thought. And yet we can't possibly
have any evidence of that. We know the world only in
thought and so can know it only *as* thought. We have
no reason, then, not to think—and every reason to
suspect—that the world does not become thought in
us, but rather is already, in itself, thought."

"And the difference it would make for how we see
reality is…?"

Roland, evidently fully back in the present now,
stared at me somewhat incredulously. "Surely you know
the answer to that already."

"I suppose I do," I admitted.

"In fact, what difference would it *not* make? It would
mean, for instance, that many of the things we call the
cosmological argument for the reality of God could
not be easily dismissed as crude attempts to argue for
a God of the gaps, but must instead be confronted as
arguments regarding logical contingency and logical
necessity. It would…well, it would have implications
for the issue of whether the concept of a *prima causa*
really occupies the same nonsensical logical and ontological space as the utterly useless concept of a *causa
sui*, as Schopenhauer believed it did. It would *certainly*
have implications for our understanding of the place
of mind in nature—or, for that matter, vice-versa."

"Naturally…"

"At the deepest level, however"—and here Roland
turned his eyes directly toward mine, and the bright-
ness of the moonlight was intense enough to illuminate
the solemn expression on his face even against the
pallid glare of the computer screen behind him—"it
has implications for whether we are ever really in

communion with the world around us. If reality were simply Galileo's qualityless realm of mass, velocity, and brute force — if all causality were mere mechanical efficiency, mere matter and force in the modern sense of those terms, divorced from form and finality — then we would only ever be in communion with ourselves... except that, of course, not even that would be true, since we would be only representations to ourselves, as much as to anyone else, psychological characters in a drama played out in our inner theater of representation. If the world and mind do not participate together, according to their diverse modes, in a single real order of forms and ends — and therefore also of real qualities and intrinsic coherences — what are we but exiles from being, protected from the barren glare of the noumenon of Kant's transcendental deduction by a delicately woven veil of illusion? But if there are, say, real formal causes, both noetic and ontological — since that is a distinction without a difference, it turns out — and all efficient and material forces exist only as inseparably united to such forms, and if by virtue of the indistinction between the ontological and the gnoseological those same forms inhabit our minds, then the world and our consciousness of it really coincide in the *nuptial* event of knowledge...and of love. We exist in an order of analogically related causalities — *aitiai* — and that order is one ontological and noetic act."

For more than a minute, silence reigned between us. I turned my eyes to the window and noted that the rays of the moon's light were now entering it at more of an acute angle than when I had first awoken.

"You know I agree with all of that," I finally said, "though I lack your skill in saying it."

Once again, a kind smile came to Roland's lips and eyes. "Among primates, yours is a promising species," he said.

"That's very gracious of you."

"That reminds me," he said, "I found another of your Great Uncle Aloysius's poems."

This at once diverted me from the train of thoughts into which I was beginning to drift. "Really? How? From when?"

"Some old letters of his had got mixed in with some files of yours that escaped the general purge back in 2014, and in one of them — a letter he wrote to an editor of a poetry magazine but then apparently never mailed — was a long three-page poem from 1956, typed on onionskin. Very carefully typed, for that matter, as the whole thing is center-rectified, which means he must have had to count the spaces in each line and calculate the margins... Curious that he decided not to submit it, if that's what happened."

"What's it about?"

Roland's expression became somewhat wry, and he sighed. "You know, that's never the proper thing to ask about a poem."

"Yes, yes," I said. "But what's it about?"

He shrugged. "I think it's his *Intimations of Immortality*. It's called 'Orphic Fragments,' and it definitely has something of... something of an esoteric quality to it... hermetic. It seems to be about birth and death and rebirth. But at one point it seems to be about... well, about *this*, what we've just been talking about... about whether the real world is the world known to mind... to *spirit*, or whether... Well, would you care to see it?"

"Of course," I replied.

"It's on the desktop," he said as he lightly leapt down from the chair: "the PDF file entitled 'OFbyAB.'" He stretched and sauntered toward the window and seated himself below the sill, gazing outward and upward to the moon; and all at once — bathed as he was in the pure, glistening light, and not now contorting his features with antic grins and seductive twinkles of the eye — I could see that indeed he looked quite elegant in that fedora. But I also saw and recognized his normal air of serene detachment, and I could not quite dispel the impression that the light was somehow emanating from him, like the light of holiness.

I found and opened the file. The images of typewritten pages were so clear that I could make out the shape of a watermark on one page and could tell easily where, in one or two places, my great uncle had whited out a word and re-typed it. This is what I read:

## ORPHIC FRAGMENTS

### I

See now this wakened exile from the dark
Go forth again into the gently shining world;
See then the vast estate of oceans, lands, and skies,
Beneath a canopy of clouds unfurled
Across the lunar heaven, once again arise;
And see these glorious mountains looming stark
Against the Milky Way
As it streams downward to the glittering horizon.
Those soft sidereal lights can dazzle newborn eyes
That still, as yet, have never seen the day,
And will not see it till the dawn's light — rising
Through a drifting rain
That softly taps upon the windowpane

And falls upon white petals damp with dew—
At last shines out alone
Upon that new
And innocent young flesh, compounded on soft bone.

## II

An image from a dream—
A flower in the desert and
The shadow of an outstretched hand
Poised to pluck it from its arid bed—
Becomes instead
A dream of armies in the night
That build their fires along the shores
(So many that it seems the stars have come to earth),
And fix their wills on endless wars,
And pitch their dark innumerable tents
Where clouds of glowing ash before the spume
Assume
A golden splendor and a ghostly eminence.
But then the morning tide, a beam
Of silver light,
And cries of gulls rouse you from sleep
As day is brought to birth
And drives the vision far away, like a storm
That breaks above the gray tormented deep
And bears all things into a flight of form.

## III

Stand still upon the morning shore
And watch the white seabirds that soar
Above the ramparts of the dawn,
And see the tide that breaks upon the strand,
And listen to the hollow
Voices of the gliding turquoise waves,
And glimpse the frigid light that mad men follow

Down to their silent, dark, unfathomed graves,
And pray for all who now are gone.
Pray also that the shallow light that dwells
Upon the water's glass-green swells
Amid those flickering emerald gleams
Where surfaces give way
To depth on depth, and some
Subaqueous sleeping titan dreams
The coming day—
Pray *these* will prove to be the very forms of things,
Known truly by the mind that gazes
on those flashing wings.
Pray the prayer of bone and clay:
That the improbable will withstand
All rational reduction and
Continue to be coral, wind, and sand,
And motion in the blossoms of the trees,
And fire in the shadows of the seas.

IV

You do not know or clearly see
What moves beyond the window and the broken gate,
And through the shade beneath the bending tree,
And yet you wait,
Expecting some grand revelation.
You cannot know
The changeless source of transformation
Or what still depths, unseen but always felt,
Bear all things up from far below,
Supporting all your idle wanderings.
While the hours melt,
You stray,
Lured on by blanching light and empty sound,
But never touch the deep, abiding ground.

And yet the promise of the sapphire sky
Emerging from the golden light of dawning day
Still calls to you.
All things still call to you:
The changing lights upon the surface of the deep
Above the secrets that the sea-beds keep,
The eagle's distant lacerating cry,
The songs of birds among the trees,
The gold enigma of the fruit upon the boughs that sway
Against the tender breeze,
The silent stars that turn upon their pole
And each bright facet of the whole
That draws the mind and with it draws desire
Into the one eternal dance of living fire.


V

See at the last the weary exile of the night
Go from the shining world into the dark once more;
And watch the hectic flight
Of autumn's leaves against the darkening sky;
And gaze up to the mountain ridges where
The last flames of the daylight die
Into the glow of the green crepuscular air.
The breath of life has now grown weak in you,
The dry, delirious soul is nearly spent;
You walk upon the fragrant forest floor
Among the ruby shadows of the needles scattered there,
But do not pray,
For it was from the silence you were sent
Into the contrapuntal music of the earth,
And to the silence that you now return
To wait upon another birth
Beyond the regions where the fixed stars burn.
The furtive dusk approaches as the long day ends,

And on that far horizon thronged with pines
A luminous, transparent blue descends
And fills with ghostly whispers and faint signs
Of glory hidden in the folds of night;
The gold and emerald and red expose
The evening's depths; the spirit roves
Past darkness and the fountainhead of light.


When I had finished reading, I said nothing for several moments. I re-read the ending lines of the third and the fifth cantos. Then I was again silent, for about twenty seconds perhaps. "I don't know," I said at last, "maybe he decided something was still missing, and that's why he didn't..." — but here I turned the chair about to address Roland only to discover that he was no longer there. He had quietly departed the room while I was reading. He had left the fedora behind, however, neatly resting in the center of my pillows.

What happened next has slipped my memory, but I imagine I soon went back to sleep, this time in my own bed.

# Roland on the Need for Repression

THIS TIME IT was the moon that woke me, I believe. At least, when I opened my eyes, I found myself awash in its light, pouring in through the uncurtained window above the daybed where I had fallen asleep; and, on turning my gaze slightly to my right and upward, I found myself staring at it directly, low in the dark blue sky, dazzling in its mensal fullness. Even so, somehow—whether on account of some subtle evidence available to my senses but not to my conscious mind or on account of something of a more psychical nature—I knew that I was not alone. Turning my eyes to the left, I saw my dog Roland seated on the floor very nearby and staring intently at me. In the lunar light, there was something slightly preternatural about his appearance; the white portions of his coat glistened icily, while its darker shades (mahogany and charcoal and gray) seemed richer and warmer than usual; and his glossy coal-black nose and limpid brown eyes shone now with a mysterious beauty. He neither moved nor made any sound.

Breathing deeply, I raised my head from the pillows, swung my legs about, sat up, and placed my feet on the floor. Now my eyes met his. After a moment, I said, "What am I doing here?"—expecting no answer.

But Roland did answer, in that familiar voice of his (so much like Laurence Harvey's): "You were reading and fell asleep" — with a slight tilt of his snout he indicated a book lying on the floor beside the bed (*Where Three Roads Meet* by Salley Vickers) — "and the night fell while you were sleeping, and then the chaste goddess of the moon crept up furtively from the horizon and came upon you here, supine and at her mercy."

I raised my hands to my head and ran their fingers through my hair — what there is of it — and attempted a smile. "Happily she's merciful by nature."

"Maybe," Roland replied. "But I have to admit that, whenever I see her in this aspect, I feel an almost irrepressible desire to bark at her and to howl, and not to stop until she's departed again." He lowered his head and shook it gently side to side, as if quietly amused. "We can none of us entirely extirpate our aboriginal natures from ourselves. It's an impulse that no doubt stretches back into the deepest abyss of my immemorial ancestral lupine past."

"No doubt."

"Mind you," he said, looking up into my eyes again, "it's not only that. I mean, it's not only an irrational impulse. At a deep level — albeit not so deep that I can't fathom it — it's an impulse of pure piety...of worship and adoration...and of communion with the deep dreaming mind that dwells behind all things, and that reveals itself in these shining symbols of its creative power...these tokens of love."

I felt my eyes widen at this. "We seem to be diving into the metaphysical deep end rather quickly," I remarked. "I'm not quite awake yet, you know."

He sighed. "Sorry," he said. "But it's something all dogs naturally understand, of course. I mean, they understand that all of reality is composed of signs

and symbols—of forms of communication and communion—and that certain of those signs and symbols
must naturally evoke a response. It's not our instincts
alone that tell us to lift up our voices in devotion and
adulation; more vitally it's our souls that do so. It's an
eros for the good, a yearning for that which is most
high...and that's what prompts our songs. Still, out
of courtesy to you and the rest of the family, I refrain
from pouring out the hymnody that wants so ardently
to spring to my lips. Repression, after all, is the price
of civil harmony."

"I see," I murmured. "That's exceedingly kind of you.
Not that we want to inhibit your nature..." I noticed
a wry smirk appear on his face at this. "So," I added,
a little self-consciously, "what were you doing here?
Why were you watching me?"

"Oh..." he shrugged. "Mostly morbid fascination."

"Morbid..."

"There's something so enchantingly...well, so enchantingly *graceless* about the way primates sleep. The slack
jaw and open mouth, the salivatory effusions, the ster-
torous snorts and gasps and rattles, the..."

"Ah, yes," I interrupted, "I see."

"The snivels and nasal whines..."

"Yes," I said more emphatically. "I understand. You
needn't go on." I rubbed my eyes. "That's why people
generally don't like being watched when they sleep."

"And yet Mama," he continued, as if I had said nothing worth acknowledging, "sleeps with an altogether
angelic serenity...like a marble image of a goddess...
one carved with the artistry of a Praxiteles."

"Well, I admit she's not given to my... *dramatic* respi-
ratory tendencies. At least, I've been told that I..."

"She does everything with ineffable grace," said Roland. "Even when she's making no effort to do anything at all. But you..." He turned a look on me that hovered disquietingly between melancholy and malevolence. "There are hurricanes with more self-control."

"I have a lung condition, you know," I weakly protested.

His expression became gentler. "I know," he said. "I was there when you fell ill. I know also that we can control only what we can control. I know it's unintentional...however insufferable it may be."

I could think of nothing to say.

"As long as we control the things we can and should control, these involuntary disturbances of the peace can be pardoned. You can't help it, after all, if your simian nature gravitates ineluctably toward the slovenly and grotesque."

"Now, hold on..."

"No offense intended," he added, momentarily leaning forward and lightly licking the back of my hand. "I don't object to apish ungainliness. Only to some kinds of apish behavior. The sort of things one finds on the internet, for instance. I mean...well, I recently opened a Twitter account."

I looked at him to see whether he appeared to be joking, but his face betrayed nothing. "You?" I asked.

"Well..." He rose from his haunches, stretching himself forward and then backward, yawning, and then seating himself again and briefly nibbling at one of his rear thighs. "Needless to say, I used your Gmail account."

"Mine?" I was appalled. "You know how I feel about social media. You know I find it all revolting."

"As do I," said Roland. "I feel the same. But it occurred

to me that neither of us has any actual experience on which to base our revulsion. So I thought, as a sort of experiment, I might try it out for a month, to see if it's quite as horrid as we assume."

"But why my...?"

"I prefer anonymity," he interrupted. "You — well, you're a public exhibitionist already, aren't you? Anyway, surely anything I might have written could only redound to your credit." He looked at me with an impish smile, but I knew he was not entirely jesting. "I confess I did on one or two occasions let slip that I was your dog, but it was generally taken as some sort of witticism on your part. Anyway, I left the account open for a month, engaged in a few exchanges with the good, the bad, and the spiritually deformed, then closed it down again. As I understand, when one closes such an account one's little messages eventually vanish. So I doubt there's even a trace of your presence left on the platform."

"Your presence, you mean."

"Where I am, there you are too," he said. "I have to confess, it was enlightening — if not in a nice way."

"As bad as we imagine?" I asked.

"Yes, sometimes. Sometimes not. There were some reasonable and even very intelligent persons online, and they made comments that were not at all offensive. But there were others who made me tremble with sorrow for your species — and terror for every other species. From behind the skirts of the sane and genial the mad and truculent began to emerge, and then to appear in ever greater numbers. They...well, I won't repeat some of the abusive and paranoid and frankly fascistic non-sense that some of them began spouting. Many were deeply stupid, many deeply demented, but the most frightening were neither — they were merely evil, and proud of it." He shook his head lugubriously, breathed deeply, and then stared directly me. The moonlight was an uncanny fire in his eyes.

I picked up the novel I had been reading from the floor and set it down beside me. "It's not as if the internet created human...fractiousness."

He smiled faintly. "I know that there are misapprehensions and conflicts in every era. Things fall apart, things go awry, things miss their mark. Such is the nature of *things* — such is the nature of entropy. Order is always a transient resistance to disorder, while disorder remains the ineluctable destiny of every physical system, however simple. In the past, a telegram might fail to be delivered, a letter might be posted in the wrong envelope, an overheard remark might be radically misconstrued and lead to resentments. But those are all mistakes, accidents, misunderstandings. What's so terrible about this medium — these media, rather — is that they cultivate *too much* understanding...they rob you of necessary illusions. In the past, lines of communication were always obstructed...always salubriously impeded. Custom and courtesy and comity taught everyone except the sociopathic some degree of restraint. Social censure was still a powerful deterrent. And then there was the sheer physical difficulty of communication at large and across great distances. For one's views to be published abroad, one had to...well, to *publish*. And that meant clambering over the many obstacles of editors and critics and in many cases censorship, legal or merely prudential. But now you've arrived at a state of perfect public transparency. On the one hand, you've abandoned the intricate rules of civic continency...reserve...

useful inhibition. On the other, you've been given a technology that allows you instantaneous global reach for whatever impulsive thought springs into your minds and breaches the barriers of your lips before you can catch hold of them…or the barriers of your fingertips, I suppose—or thumbs…though I have no personal experience in that sphere…" He looked away toward a shadowy corner, clearly lost in thought.

"Well," I said, "what can one do? Better not to fret."

He seemed not to have heard me. "No wonder your politics have become so savage and deranged. No wonder so many pliant minds have fallen under the spells of beasts and barbarians. No wonder violence has become so prevalent in your political and social life. You poor simian brutes—you simply don't have the neurological capacities needed to use a technology so monstrously powerful—needed to exist safely in so pitilessly transparent a medium—naked in the blazing glare of public exposure. If you were dogs, then of course there would be no danger. You would possess the spiritual resources to govern your more bestial impulses. But you apes— well, you require…delay…the mediation of the opaque and indirect and oblique. You require ceremonies of innocence to hold your diseased urges in confinement." Finally, he returned his gaze to mine. "The price of civilization is repression. Freud had at least that much right. Society survives principally through the preservation of judicious silences, prudent abstinences, nimble evasions, artful ambiguities. Let not light in upon the mystery. But now, nothing is hidden. You're now the creatures of this malignant transparency you've created. All those glistening veils of custom and courtesy, of benign dissemblance and decorous insincerity, as well as all those layers of technical postponement and editorial scrutiny, have been torn utterly away, exposing the naked essences of your souls — in all their horrible, unguarded spontaneities and ebullitions — to one another. Now every private psychopathy is rendered visible to every other. As I say, for dogs this would be no peril at all. But for you — for you it's nothing less than the collapse of your civilization, the end of civil life. Your society simply has no hope of surviving such a technology. By the way, someone online accused you of cultural appropriation, because you write about Asian literature and art and such, though you aren't Asian. It wasn't only the crazed religious traditionalists who were out to get you."

I could not suppress a small groan. "When I was young, you know, cross-cultural appreciation was generally seen as a very good thing...even a virtue. And I always thought of the intermingling of cultures as... well, as *civilization*...a word that in my experience only fascists detest."

He nodded. "Yes, I know," he said. "What's the line from Terence? *Simius sum, simiani nihil a me alienum puto.* A very noble sentiment." He looked away again, this time toward the moon.

"Yes, something like that," I said after a few seconds. I turned my eyes in the same direction. For nearly three minutes, neither of us spoke. Then, at last, I asked, "Would you care for some treats?"

"That sounds like a good idea," he replied. "By the way, that's my copy of *Where Three Roads Meet* that you're reading."

"Is it? I..."

"The author sent it to me herself, with a personal inscription."

I looked at him, once again trying to discern whether he was joking. And, as before, there was no sign that he was. I picked up the book and opened it to the title page, and even in the moonlight I could see the words of the handwritten note and signature, in thin strokes of sepia ink. Salley had indeed sent it to Roland, not to me. "I'm sorry," I said, "I should have asked. I didn't even know you two were friends."

"I do have a life of my own," he said.

"Again, I'm sorry."

"That's all right," he said. "I've borrowed enough of your books without asking. Shall we get those treats then?"

I set the novel aside, rose from the bed, and walked to the door of the room, but as I opened it I realized that Roland had not yet followed me. I turned to see him still sitting there in the middle of the floor, staring through the window at the brilliant full moon floating over the dark line of trees beyond. He seemed to be trembling ever so slightly. Then, all at once, he lifted his mouth, stretched out his throat, parted his lips, and emitted a long, loud, ululating howl that persisted for fully half a minute, rising and falling in register, and terminating in a terse, shrill bark. Then he lowered his head, rose to his feet, and turned to face me with a somewhat bashful expression on his face.

I stared at him with as impassive a look as could muster, trying not to laugh. Then I said — again, attempting to contain my mirth — "And you speak of restraint."

He shrugged. "One must occasionally yield to nature. That too is necessary for civilization. As long as it does no harm." And with that he trotted past me and through the door, out into the unlit corridor.

3

# Roland on
# Creative Evolution

## (ROLAND IN THE MORNING, PART 1)

I COULD TELL THAT it was early morning. The sunlight slipping in through the half-opened jalousies of my home office's window had that soft, gauzy quality it takes on just after dawn on clear days. I did not, however, remember how or why I had come into the room, or even whether I had just risen from bed or had been up and about for some time. I realized after a moment that I was in my dressing gown; I was also carrying a large cup full of coffee, still very hot, though I could not recall having poured it; but I had no memory of having wakened from sleep. This was not a new experience for me, though. I suffer from a condition I vaguely call "oneirolepsy," which causes my conscious mind occasionally to shift, without my noticing the transition, into a kind of lucid dreaming, and which is invariably bracketed by moments of disorientation when I am never quite certain whether I am emerging from or sinking into the waking dream. For several seconds, I could not decide which was the case just then. When, however, I took a sip of my coffee and immediately recognized it as a very rich Ethiopian Yirgacheffe, I concluded that I must be fully conscious, as my senses are never that acute when I am in one of my oneiric states. I took a second sip. Then I noticed Roland: he was lying on his side on the daybed in the corner of the room, seemingly fast asleep; he had somehow contrived to draw the dark red counterpane as well as a throw blanket over his back and eyes, and what was visible of his snout suggested a state of deep contentment. I smiled, as I always do on first catching sight of him in the morning, seated myself as quietly as I possibly could in my desk chair, and swiveled it around so that I could continue to look at him.

Only a moment passed, however, before he spoke — though without moving his head or opening his eyes. "I've been editing the galleys for your forthcoming book," he murmured: "you know, the one on mind, life, and language." His voice, as ever, reminded me of Laurence Harvey's, though at this register it suggested one of Harvey's later roles (perhaps the murderous chess-master he played in that episode of *Columbo*).

I sighed and took a full swallow of the coffee. "I can never be stealthy enough not to wake you, can I?"

I saw the corner of his mouth drawn up into a smile. "You're at a considerable disadvantage on that score. I have an auditory apparatus honed by unimaginably vast epochs of evolutionary refinement into an instrument of astonishing sensitivity, subtlety, and range…"

"True…" I began.

"…to say nothing of my olfactory faculty…"

"Of course."

"…whereas you, sadly, are the phylogenic residue of a tragically degenerate simian line…"

"Now, there's no need…"

"…one that long ago lost its tail, shed its nimbleness and, alas, acquired the ungainly and unbalanced somatic *Bauplan* needed to accommodate that grotesque neoteny that has made your species so singularly adept at warfare, unprincipled scheming, and sonnets. It would be all but impossible for you not to rouse me when you come slouching and shambling into a room, no matter how soundly I might be sleeping. To ears as acutely perceptive as mine, your footfalls might as well be an avalanche in an echoing mountain pass." He paused for a moment, in that way he does whenever an interesting thought occurs to him. Then he lifted his head, causing the covers to fall back, and stared at me with an expression that seemed delicately to combine whimsy with pity. "It's strange, you know. Evolution is such a capricious process. It so often favors adaptations that conduce to one evolutionary advantage only at the cost of thwarting another. Not always, of course. Sometimes, a perfect balance is struck, as is ever the case with dogs, in whose evolutionary history every emergent physical capacity has been associated with an equally impressive mental and moral advance. Sometimes, however, as in the case of squirrels, the acquisition of new powers that enhance the chance of survival — say, low cunning, powerful but hideous incisors, a hardened habit of furtiveness and malice — are paid for by a loss of equal or even greater powers that might have led to higher developments of the species — say, moral intelligence, rationality...tails with dignified shapes rather than vulgar appendages that resemble ragged dust-mops or tattered feather-boas..." He paused again, seeming to have become momentarily lost in thought.

"I think you shouldn't..." I began.

"I mean," he abruptly resumed, "horseshoe crabs and lobsters long ago took a path toward survival that terminated in the development of an arthropodal panoply to defend them against predators; it was an elegant solution to the precariousness of life, and an economical one too, in a significant sense; but it was costly in another sense, since once they were sealed within their brittle armatures their phylogenic potentials more or less came to an unceremonious halt. By refusing to remain exposed to the savage artistry of natural selection, with all its wanton disregard for the perishable and fragile phenotype, they condemned themselves to genotypic stagnation. That's why horseshoe crabs have produced so very few distinguished philosophers or dramatists...no more than two or three, to be honest. It's true of plant-life too in some ways, with its fibrous external tissues; many vegetal lines have come to an evolutionary end in a state of perpetual organic somnolence. There's nothing wrong with that, but each of them is a strain within the music of creation that's had a dying fall. Life's poetic genius at its most irrepressibly innovative requires semipermeable boundaries in which

to work its esemplastic and metamorphic miracles...
pellicles rather than shells...involucra rather than plate-
mail...pervious and ever imperiled membranes rather
than chitinous corselets or cellulose sheathes. The mad
and gallant artistry of life demands that the organism
abandon itself and its posterity to danger...to hazard...
to the cast of the dice." He breathed deeply, and perhaps a bit morosely. "But life must learn that lesson for
herself, I suppose. Isis, uncouth goddess that she is—or
Psyche, let's call her, or Inanna, or Rhea crowned with
towers—well, it's ever her fate to search along all the
byways and secret paths...the country lanes hidden
among the flowering hawthorns...till she reaches the
end and must turn back...." He fell silent.

"It's considerate of you to edit my galleys for me," I
volunteered after several seconds, "but it's not really..."

"Really," he said, "how nonsensical it is to imagine that evolution advances only through strategies of
ever more sheltered, local, and structurally efficient
persistence and survival. Natural selection merely con-
serves and curates; left to itself, it would craft only
durable mediocrity out of the commonest genetic clay.
But evolution in itself is supreme creativity, supreme
inspiration...supreme divine mania...and that means
courting the most extreme jeopardies, unfurling one's
sails into the driving gales of chance, hazarding everything on that throw of the dice—again and again and
again, relentlessly. It's the insatiable desire to be, and to
be more, and to aspire ever upwards toward the all—
to become God, in fact—that's the true unwearying
dynamo driving the ceaseless generation of species.
The *conatus essendi*—the *conatus adsurgendi*, if I might
coin a phrase—there's the dance of Dionysus—there's

the delirium of beauty, the inebriate orgy of spiritual yearning, the force that through the green fuse drives the flower...that surges upward from the very cells composing us toward the great eternal act of thought that comprises all being in itself. And it advances only through a...through a lovingly cultivated *fragility*— a tenderness of structure that's also an openness to illimitable futurity. In evolutionary terms, the slug is mightier than the snail!"

He pronounced this last with so triumphant an intonation that I was unable for a moment to reply. When I did, moreover, all I could think to say was: "I wouldn't have thought slugs wanted to be gods more than snails do."

"And yet evidently they do," he said. "They declare it in their touching helplessness. Or, at least, the primal desire to become gods is more creatively at work in their cells and organic systems than in those of their somewhat more phylogenically cautious cousins. Really, it seems obvious to me that we shouldn't doubt for a moment the divine passions and fervors that constantly rise up in their sluggish little hearts—that heaven-scaling, reckless delight in the flight into the abyss of possibility. Every slug incubates within itself a little Daedalus—a little Icarus...or a Phaethon. Deep in the womb of every slug's soul, a god slumbers...a soft, sebaceous, daintily slimy little god, true, but a god all the same. I quite like slugs."

"I see."

"Mind you, I quite like snails too. And I have to admit that their shells have a disconcertingly evocative fragrance sometimes—something one can't quite place one's toenail on, but endlessly suggestive. And, on the whole, they're more cheerfully garrulous than slugs, who tend a bit more toward somber simplicity and taciturnity."

"Have you had many conversations with snails, then?"

"It's almost as if," he continued, taking no notice of my question, "at every fork in the evolutionary road, life has to make a calculated choice. It has to decide which powers may be shed so that others may flourish...may hypertrophy, one might even say...as if in its need to persist and flourish it's always being confronted by the option of either cultivating further physical and spiritual potencies, even at the risk of rendering itself more vulnerable to predators and more prone to structural deformations — you know, the way your primate line settled on tiny teeth, weak jaws, tiny brittle talons, glabrous skin, pathetically impotent noses, and so forth, simply in order to force its somatic dynamisms into a more cerebrally capacious and synaptically complex organism — or instead choosing the safer path of a stabler and more perdurable but far more limited accommodation with its environment." Now his eyes met mine, and he seemed to be hesitating to say something.

I arched an eyebrow inquisitively.

He took a deep breath, half rose from the bed, turned about, and lay down again, now on his other side. "The truth is," he said at last, "that I gave up on the editing after a couple hundred pages. I should have inserted myself into the composition of the book at an earlier stage when...well, when I might perhaps have been able..." He paused, pursed his lips, and then breathed deeply again.

"Yes...?" I prompted him after several seconds of uncomfortable silence.

He looked at me with a wanly whimsical grimace. "I would perhaps have suggested a few cuts...a little rearrangement of the material...perhaps an entirely different form of exposition..." He gave one of his front paws a few slow, meditative licks and then lightly nibbled at one of his toes. "Oh," he added nonchalantly, "and I might have radically...well, let's say, *sharpened* the central argument. I don't mean to sound needlessly critical, but..." He did not go on.

I took a longer swallow of my coffee and then attempted a smile of my own. "It was always really your project," I said. "You were the one who wrote the original proposal, as I recall. If you weren't so jealous of your privacy—or of your anonymity, to be more accurate—you could have written and published it under your own name."

He shook his head indulgently. "You're so naïve. There are such prejudices..." He raised his eyes to mine again. "Anyway, it's as much your argument as mine. I did, after all, compose the proposal from notes you'd taken, so..." He knitted his brows. "I do have a question, though, one that's apposite to what I was just saying about life choosing its evolutionary paths. You do go on quite a bit in the book about organisms being composed of 'cognitive systems all the way down' and such, and about the inseparability of the various dimensions of mental agency—cognition, intentionality, consciousness, will, ratiocination, representation, subjectivity, and so on—but it seems to me you leave one crucial question painfully obscure."

I waited for him to say more, but soon realized that he was going to force me to ask him to do so. "Yes?" I finally said. "What's that?"

"Do you think that cells…organic cells, I mean… do you think that they… *think*?"

"Think?"

"You know — make plans, cherish hopes and desires…form opinions, choose courses of action… contemplate their existence — *think*. If they possess real agency, even mentality of some kind…?"

"Oh, I see." I drank some more of my coffee. "No, I don't imagine that every cell is invested with personal consciousness in the way that human beings… or, rather, in the way that you and I are. I simply believe that all of life — every level of life — participates in higher and fuller levels of intentionality and…and creative intelligence…and that all of it participates in one great…in one *infinite* act of thought…thought thinking thought, or the thinking of thinking…" Roland was now staring at me more intently than I found entirely encouraging, but I continued: "I suppose I'd say that every level of life, from the most advanced of organisms down to the most primitive cellular processes — if you'll forgive me putting it that way — is given its form and finality by a more supereminent source of mental agency, and each level, the human included — or, rather, the human and the canine — participates in that source in its own mode, and in its own degree of intensity and integration. I mean, the cells of my body participate as cognitive systems within the larger intentionality of my organism, which itself is at a higher level of agency formed and guided by my conscious mind…" Now Roland was narrowing his eyes. "And all of it — all of us — everything — we live and move and have our being in the one great mind that is the thinking of all that…"

"Yes," he interrupted, "I understand. And hence your impatience with what might be called 'bottom-up panpsychism' — panpsychism of the physicalist variety, that is. As I thought." He ran his tongue over his nose slowly, pensively. "Mind descends through the countless fathoms of the ocean of life, down to the uttermost dim and dismal depths of matter, while nature rises up continuously and ecstatically toward the sunlit surface above, and toward the pure light of spirit, and these two movements are one. As ever, ὁδὸς ἄνω κάτω μία καὶ ὡυτή. Something one hears out on the streets every day. I agree, of course, although I'd caution you not to underestimate the intelligence of organic cells. For all you know, they like to compose little poems and songs as they go about their work. All the evidence suggests, after all, that they're very cooperative and communal by nature, and surely that indicates some kind of social intelligence at the very least."

"Well, I suppose…"

"I simply think it's best not to assume. All sorts of bigotries take shape when one does. But that's neither here nor there. As I was saying — as far as you're concerned, then, mental agency can't be an emergent phenomenon in any strong sense, but is 'emergent' only in the sense that any particular line of organic evolution can come to participate with ever greater intensity in higher levels of mentality, higher levels of formal causality. That is, for any line of phylogeny, mentality progressively 'emerges' only in the sense that it explicates an innate capacity, the organism's inmost potentiality, and does so to the degree that the organism surrenders itself to life, so that that potency can be actualized ever more…ever more extravagantly. Again, that rules out bottom-up panpsychism, because you won't allow that some sort of primordial and aimless and non-intentional consciousness could, just as a matter of fortuity, become a truly purposive agency—a true intentionality—as that would entail the sudden appearance within physical nature of a transcendental horizon beyond anything immediate, somehow recognizable to organic systems as a value to be pursued. Rather, for you, any such intentionality would have to be preceded by an always more original desire, one within whose embrace all finite desires—all directed actions of the will toward intentional ends under finite aspects—are prompted into actuality. Yes?"

"I've said as much," I replied. "More to the point, I don't believe in consciousness entirely devoid of intentionality, or of cognition entirely devoid of consciousness. I think all the dimensions of mind are present wherever real mental agency exists; they're present, obviously, in varying degrees of relative intensity, but nothing can dissolve their essential unity with one another."

"Yes, yes…" said Roland, pausing to open his jaws in a sudden and grandly ostentatious yawn. "Excuse me," he said when he had finished. "I was up late working on those blasted galleys. You realize, of course, that what you're saying isn't simply contrary to the philosophical temper of the time—I mean, it's hardly a startling piece of news that Neoplatonism and vitalism and so forth are all out of fashion, especially among the self-appointed clerisy of the Anglophone world—but, more to the point, what you're saying is largely inconceivable under the present intellectual regime. None of the reigning philosophical paradigms can accommodate it—nor can the prejudices of the age. And, of course, I needn't tell you why that is."

"No, indeed," I said, nodding sagely. "The triumph of the mechanical philosophy."

"Well, yes, of course," he said, with an exceedingly gentle — though perhaps slightly condescending — smile, "but I was thinking more particularly about the most obvious problem of all: to wit, the modern world's impoverished ontology of time."

"Oh," I said; and then, after a second or two, I added an unconvincing "*That* — of course."

Roland stared at me with a fond and very patient expression in his eyes, but he said nothing.

"Oh, all right," I yielded after only a few seconds of this, "you'll have to explain what you mean by that."

His smile became at once even kinder but also craftier. "Certainly, but you may want to fill your cup again before we start."

"I think I left the press downstairs," I said.

"No," he replied, "it's there on your desk, just behind you."

I turned my head and saw that he was right.

*To be continued…*

# 4

# Roland on Time's Hierarchy

## (ROLAND IN THE MORNING, PART 2)

WHEN I HAD filled my cup again and taken a swallow of my coffee, I swiveled my chair about only to be met by the sight of Roland — still languorously recumbent atop the throw blanket — training a particularly gimlet eye upon me.

"What?" I asked after a moment. "Why are you staring at me like that?"

At once his expression softened. "Excuse me," he said. "I was only looking to see whether I could make out the wheels turning in your head, so to speak. I thought you might be working out what I mean by an 'ontology of time.'"

"Oh," I replied, "it's still too early for that." I raised my cup to my lips. "And I haven't had enough coffee yet." I took another swallow.

Roland sighed. "A reliance on stimulants, you know, can only lead to the atrophy of the natural faculties. That's what did in the Inca civilization, you know — too much chewing of coca leaves on long afternoons... especially in the higher elevations of Peru, where the air's thin."

"I'm not sure that's true," I said, feeling my brow furrow. "Anyway, three-quarters of my intelligence is pure caffeine. You wouldn't find my conversation worth your time if it weren't for coffee and tea."

He continued to stare at me, but now with a look of mild concern in his eyes. "It was chocolate that brought down the Aztec Empire, you know. Too much theobromine...and too much human sacrifice, of course, as that tends to ruffle people's feathers."

"It wasn't because of the *conquistadores*?"

"Those too." He licked his shoulder twice or thrice meditatively. "Anyway, just a word to the wise." He paused suddenly, mid-slather, and darted an inquisitive glance at me. "You understand I'm not actually suggesting that the people of that time had feathers, even if ancient Mesoamerican sacral vestments did occasionally use the borrowed plumage of exotic birds?"

I nodded. "Yes, I understood the metaphor."

"I ask only because I'm not sure how firm your grasp of all the details of evolutionary theory is."

"Good enough for that, I hope. And I suppose you know best about chocolate and coffee, but I'm hopelessly addicted to the latter. As to the matter at hand, though, you say modern philosophy — modern Anglophone philosophy, at least — can't accommodate my... my what? My animism or vitalism or panpsychism, I suppose."

Roland smiled gently. "Yes, the name is hard to settle on, isn't it? 'Idealism in an animist vein,' perhaps."

"And this is chiefly because it presumes a defective ontology of time?"

"That's my story and I'm sticking to it."

"Yes," I said, "so I gather. But you've yet to explain what you mean."

For several seconds, he gazed away at the pale morning light streaming in through the half-opened blinds, his lips pursed. Then, turning his eyes back to mine, he said, "I don't mean to generalize unfairly. But so many in the analytic guild, at least among those of a rigidly materialist bent, have ordained themselves as the priesthood of the sciences—which, I suppose, makes perfect sense so long as the sciences are understood as being concerned only with a bare syntax of physical relations of mass and force. Then a philosophical method that consists in little more than atomic propositions regarding mechanical causal entailments seems somehow to conform itself naturally to the shape of reality; but surely it's wholly inadequate to the actual processes—the intentional, cognitive, creative processes—we observe at work in organic systems, precisely because it doesn't command a logical grammar that can possibly make sense of life's relation to time. Above all, it can't explain the intentional priority of the future in those processes. Really, though, hasn't this always been the problem with a mechanistic metaphysics of nature? It understands space and time only as continuous or discontinuous but serial trajectories of efficient force, moving from impulse to effect, from one event in the past to another in the present, and in regard to every moment the present exists only as the determinate result of the past. For them, in fact, the present is nothing but the past persisting in the form of a prior impulse—a prior line of force. But that's a fantasy time...time understood as a kind of Newtonian space, as Bergson would tell you, through which events and things are in movement; and, as Bergson would also tell you, even space and motion so conceived are inventions of the abstracting intellect, consisting in imaginary collections of static *heres* and *nows*, infinitely divisible points fixed within an abstract topography of pure extension. Yet, in the real order of events, we don't move through time that way — or at all, really — and the past doesn't just extend its force as a kind of momentum, in a succession of punctiliar temporal sequelae. It's just as accurate — more so, really — to say that the future is always moving backward toward us... always arriving in the present. The present's really nothing but the future arriving as the now, while the past is simply the now as the intelligible totality that's always being formed — uncovered — by that perpetual arrival of the future. And this is also to say that the now isn't a thing merely determined by the past, but rather the event of the present being... being *liberated* from the tyranny of pure force... set free to act *from* the future... and from its openness." He paused and looked away again toward the window.

After a moment, I said, "I'm very fond of Bergson's thought too." I drank more of my coffee. "I'm not necessarily any nearer, however, to understanding precisely what you..."

"Oh, yes, of course." His gaze again met mine. "Let me ask you: has it ever struck you as bizarre that those who embrace a purely physicalist account of reality seem curiously unimpressed by the causal power of meaning?"

"Of *meaning*?"

"Quite." He ran his tongue over his nose. "You're the one, after all, who likes to go on at such length about the inverse proportion of determinacy between the semantic and syntactic levels of information — or, as you would have it, from the semantic to the syntactic to the paratactic levels. Surely you recall: the lowest level becomes more random as the highest becomes more determinate, and so the higher structures can't emerge from the lower but must operate as formal causes on the physical substrate of transmission…?"

"Yes," I said, "I recall."

"And, of course, the structure of the semantic level is thoroughly intentional…?"

"Yes."

"Don't you find it rather bizarre, then, that so many persons of physicalist bent aren't at all troubled by the causal efficacy of semantic meaning? Shouldn't they be more baffled than they are by, say, the power of a written invitation to tea to produce a physical result? After all, the power of meaning lies in its sheer futurity, and that alone seems jarringly inconsistent with an uncompromisingly mechanistic picture of things. If there's a causal power in meaning, where does meaning reside? What space does it inhabit, and what's the temporal shape of that space? And, if meaning is real, how does that temporal structure interact with anything like a mechanical order of space and time?"

"Well," I said, still feeling somewhat slow of wit, "I expect that's why so many physicalist reductionists insist that intrinsic intentionality is an illusion."

A wince of pure disdain flickered briefly but vividly over Roland's features. "Which is risible gibberish," he said, "scarcely worthy of a squirrel." Then he shook his head and sighed lugubriously. "That's as may be, however. My point is of quite another kind. If you're right, after all, to lean as you do in the direction of a kind of Aristotelian aetiology in trying to make sense of the coordinated complexity of organic systems, or of an Aristotelian picture of nature as having a mindlike structure—and you are right, at least according to the most advanced schools of thought among Spaniels and Collies — and if indeed those systems are truly composed as hierarchies with numerous causal tiers, at once causally bottom-up as regards their material and efficient constraints and top-down as regards their formal and final constraints, encompassing in their totalities a logic at once mereological and systematic, then the highest, most irreducibly formal tier of life's structure is a noetic reality or order."

"I have the faintest feeling you're quoting...me, I think." I began to explore my memory but after only a few seconds abandoned the search.

"Well," said Roland, "where you are, there am I also. Another way of saying this might be that life is like music — like counterpoint, in fact: an interweaving of themes and lines of development intricately coordinated and constantly developed toward a single governing end...a single horizon of the possible...a single structure of values, sustained and continuously reiterated by the unremitting rhythm of the future's ever-repeated arrival. And music is the very epitome of temporal relations established in and by a rational finality. Even the freest of variations and improvisations flow out of a thematic and harmonic confluence of forces drawn on toward an ultimate value — an ultimate fitting and beautiful resolution — whether that end is attainable or not in the course of the performance. Or, to put it a little better perhaps, music is the epitome of the future's perpetual movement toward, and arrival in, the present." Again, his gaze wandered off in the direction of the window.

"I have to confess," I said, "I'm not quite following you."

He heaved a deep sigh. "I'm being vague, I know. I'm trying to give expression to an intuition that resolutely refuses to settle into a concrete form. I'm simply saying that, if life is indeed what it must be and mind is what mind evidently is, then not only do life and mind defy mechanistic explanation; they can't be adequately captured in the barren propositional language of analytic method. That method can't…can't carry the tune, if you know what I mean."

I took a particularly deep and satisfying swallow of coffee. "I'm disposed to agree," I said, "even without quite grasping what you're saying. I cordially loathe the analytic tradition in principle. But if you were to explain a little more fully…well…"

Now he smiled, at first in amusement and then indulgently. "Analytic method is the philosophical analogue of the mechanical philosophy: the regularization of a bare syntax of relations among isolated events and objects, and it functions best by reducing those events and objects to mere logical functions or tokens: an $x$ here, a $y$ there. It encompasses certain equations, obviously, that are perfectly useful at a very humble level of predication, but its relation to real philosophy is rather like the relation of simple arithmetic to higher mathematics. It can dissolve or aggregate, subtract or add, but analysis isn't synthesis, much less development, and it's most definitely not creativity. Yet life is all of these things, and requires a philosophical paradigm capacious enough to reflect its intrinsic strangeness. Life is music, poetry…thought. How can it be captured—how can it be glimpsed, in all its mysterious defiance of the tyranny of the past—by a purely syntactic method that, as analysis, strives essentially to reduce all synthetic truths to analytic truths…to tautologies, that is, scrupulously discriminated from one another, with all discrete terms reduced to univocities, purged of as many semantic quantities as possible, as well as purged of historical depth and analogous range and conceptual richness. Truth in that scheme is nothing more than an endless reiteration of 'A = A.' And such a philosophy is one conceived wholly in terms of a syntactic coherence that can be achieved solely by forsaking any concern for conceptual coherence. Even existence, in such a philosophy, can be thought of only as an 'existential qualifier' functioning as a second-order predicate: there is one $x$ such that $x$ is a…well, let's say a *platypus*, which is of course propositionally valid in the sense of syntactically impeccable, and yet conceptually vacuous. No" — he shook his head — "the whole analytic tradition is a tutelage in not thinking — in fact, in not knowing what thought is."

I finished the last of the coffee in my cup, turned about and filled it again, and then turned back to Roland. "Are we still talking about the ontology of time? I think I've lost the thread on that."

"Oh, yes, of course. My tendency toward *excursus* is, as you know, growing more pronounced as I age. But it's all already there in your book — even if not laid out with quite the rigor I would have preferred." He glanced at me a little apologetically but went on. "As you say there, mental agency has a 'horizontal axis,' as you phrase it — a bit unfortunately, if you ask me — a structure whose beginning and end exist each by virtue of the other. At the purely temporal level, this structure is expressed successively, but at the formal level, in a purely logical space, it exists as a rational totality, an accomplished whole logically prior to any successively ordered event. All intentional mental activity exists in that logical space first, where antecedent finality and the first efficiency, as well as integral form and materiality, are all one indiscerptible event, *sub specie aeternitatis* — as you've noted."

"All right…"

"Which is all I mean by the ontology of time. You know the Platonic maxim, the one so often inadequately rendered as 'time is the moving image of eternity,' but which of course really tells us that '*chronos* is the moving image of the *aion*': that here below the moon, in the land of unlikeness, under the reign of genesis and decay, of arising and perishing, everything is only the thin and fluent shadow of a reality that, there above, in the spheres of the heavens and within the embrace of the sphere of fixed stars, exists as pure and perfectly realized act. Of course, I'm speaking in a cosmological idiom, but that was, after all, how the matter was conceived in the antique world, in the days when no hard and fast demarcation had been drawn between the physical and the metaphysical, the cosmological and the ontological. And, needless to say, beyond the heavens and the Great Age above — beyond all the ages — there's the still higher reality of the Prime Mover or God or… or whatever." Now he smiled to himself. "Why I'm telling you things you already know I can't say. All I mean is that, in epochs when it was assumed that the structure of all of reality was mindlike, this ontology of time was necessarily presumed, and the cosmology of late antiquity was a natural imaginative translation of an essential intuition regarding the shape of all mental realities: the structure of mentality — which is also that of language, after all — was naturally expressed also as a picture of nature's physical structure, here below and there above and then even beyond the above. The 'chronic' expressions of those realities possess their unity only by virtue of that higher, logically prior 'aeonian' fullness of actuality, which itself, needless to say, exists as an integrity only by virtue of a still more eminent, more original, more transcendent and ineffable One, the changeless and simple light that shines upon the *apex intellectus*."

I made no reply, as now I was drinking from my cup in a slow, continuous series of swallows.

"All of which is to say only that, given that life and mind most definitely *are* what life and mind seem to be, and what the sciences continue to show them to be — well, in the case of life, at least, since the sciences have nothing to say about mind — no philosophy is adequate to comprehend or explain them so long as it seeks to reduce the synthetic and poetic power of both to an analytic set of tautologous simples, or so long as it fails to acknowledge and attune itself to the truth that time as we know it, rather than subsisting merely in a succession of mechanical events, is embraced in that higher logical space of values and totalities: the truth that *chronos* is embraced within an *aion* that is not divisible into past and future as discrete...discrete vectors, I suppose, and which itself is held together by a still higher and ineffable *One* beyond all ages."

"I'm only too eager to concur," I said. "When you say time as we know it, however, you don't mean time as it would be described by modern physics."

Now Roland's expression seemed to become one of faint disappointment with me. "Heaven forfend. We

don't know — don't experience — that kind of time at all.
That's a quantitative shorthand, a form of measurement
within a specific paradigm. I mean the time we experience as a present of *durée*, to use Bergson's term, in
the constant eventuation of the future. Of course, the
curious thing about that is that the intensity of that
*durée* must inevitably inflect the…the tempo, so to
speak, of the future's arrival. The time we experience
is one in which the past that the future liberates into
the fullness of the durative now seems to contract,
or rather to accelerate. The future, in a sense, arrives
at infinite speed, never delayed, never deferred, even
in its infinitely spacious openness, and as we age our
experience constantly accelerates in an attempt to catch
up to that moment of arrival…to go beyond it…to
outpace the future." He took a deep and pensive breath,
in which the slightest intonation of melancholy was
distinctly audible. "If only the pace of history were the
same as that of nature. The tragedy of the historical
now — this now, I mean, at this moment in the development of culture — is that it is increasingly inducing
in your species an experience of time that exceeds your
capacity even to reach the present instant, let alone
into the future."

I paused just as I was about to take in another draft
of coffee, and then lowered the cup from my lip. "Oh,
you must explain what you mean by that."

*To be continued…*

5

# Roland on the
# Acceleration of Experience

## (ROLAND IN THE MORNING, PART 3)

"OH," SAID ROLAND, slowly shaking his head, "I don't think I'm saying anything particularly abstruse. You know, certainly, that the way in which we experience time qualitatively isn't congruent with the way we measure time quantitatively. By the clock, a minute invariably takes sixty seconds, but in our experience of time a minute may seem either interminable or fleeting, depending on our situation, or on how the structure of retention and protention that stretches the present moment into an actual continuous now is . . . well, I suppose, how it's either strained or relaxed by states of memory, anticipation . . . trauma or ecstasy, fear or longing..."

"Yes," I said, nodding and drinking in more of my coffee.

"Time as intuited phenomenon and time as measurable magnitude are different things."

"Definitely."

"And, of course, one's sense of duration alters as one ages. Time—at least, time as an experience—accelerates as the years accumulate. Memory descries an immense ocean at its most distant horizons, mountains and valleys and prairies in the far distance, foothills and narrow terraces in the middle distance, small enclosed gardens stretching from the near distance right to its doorstep. Childhood was boundlessly vast, youth's discrete moments were full to overflowing with the promises and uncertainties of the future, early manhood was still a languid daydream of great things yet to come, possibilities yet to be realized; but then, all at once, at a threshold you never noticed crossing, the days began to pass more quickly, and then more quickly still, and then much more quickly than you had ever imagined possible. Transient experiences became ever more deliquescent, tasks displaced dreams as anxieties displaced hopes, and as your years accrued to you your sense of the present continuously contracted. And then the memories of all the things that are now irrecoverable entirely chased any expectations for the future away forever. Life is long, or so it seems until all at once you find that life is brief, and the change came on you, you realize, all in an instant you can't now recall." A strangely saturnine smile played for a moment across his features. "Consider this: if you and I are both alive a little less than a year hence, I'll have been with you for fully one-quarter of your life."

"No, surely..." I paused and made the simple calculation. "My lord," I murmured.

Now his smile became somewhat more whimsical. "Precisely. But it doesn't seem possible, does it. Set off against the endless horizon of your remembered youth, the fourteen years since I came to you — a puppy cast out upon the seas of fate, finding a safe harbor up on that mountain-top with you — well, those years probably seem to you as having elapsed in the narrow interstice between the 'only yesterday' and the 'just now.' For me it's different. For me that green and lovely Arcady was an eternal paradise that never had begun nor ever would pass away... orient and immortal wheat, as it were... and I dwelled there in unending bliss. That was the heavenly eternity from which I precipitated — fell — into time... the Eden of the Dreamtime. It was infinity."

"That *was* a happy time," I said quietly. "Or a happy timelessness... even for me." A succession of fragmentary images passed through my mind, all of them achingly tender. "Patrick was still a little fellow, always exploring the forest with me and you. You were still a puppy. The two of you were fast companions."

Roland nodded pensively. "Today, though," he said, "as I voyage into the last harbor of my senescence, I understand how it must all seem to you, who are now so far sunk in corporeal and mental decrepitude..."

"Well, wait," I said, feeling a little ill-used, "I'm still quite sharp-witted in most people's estimation. And my health has been..."

"I meant nothing by it," he said insouciantly. "I wasn't suggesting you were going senile. I was referring only to the decline of your short-term memory. I can't help but notice that it's sometimes a bit of a vexation to Mama. But I understand."

Now the shadow of a far grimmer thought passed across my mind. "You know, you're very healthy too, for a dog your age. Just a few days ago, your veterinarian said…"

"You mean," interrupted Roland, his eyes narrowing, "my *physician*. I really don't like these specious distinctions among classes of medical professionals or among classes of patients. He's a good man. I chose him with particular care as my primary care physician."

Something seemed amiss to me, but my memory refused to come to my assistance. "Are you sure it was… *you* who chose him?"

He stared at me for a moment pityingly. "It's really getting a bit cloudy up there, isn't it. Yes, of course I chose him. Do you think I'd consult just any old fellow with a framed degree on his wall? I looked into his credentials with very exacting scrutiny — his education, where he did his residency, what references he had…"

"Excuse me, did you say *residency*? Do…do vets actually have residencies?"

Now his eyes became somewhat hooded and he briefly pursed his lips. "Again, I don't approve of that word." He shook his head. "Anyway, his credentials were impeccable, and one does like to feel that one's in practiced hands. You can tell, you know. It's all in the fingertips. I can tell from how he rubs my ears — such skill, such tact…such a sense of where to apply pressure. And, despite his excellent training and academic pedigrees, there's not a hint of superciliousness in him. He has none of that *de haut en bas* manner about him that so often makes physicians who specialize in the treatment of non-human persons infuriating to deal with. I remember one who used to speak to me invariably as if I were an idiot." He knitted his brow, plainly recalling something that displeased him.

"I think we're straying a little wide of the path," I said.

"Oh, yes," he said, seeming to return to himself. "My point is that, as you age, experience accelerates...time *as* experience accelerates. I mean to say, that quarter of your existence on earth that coincides with practically my entire existence on earth seems to you like only a small part of your life because the time you now experience in these later years of your life isn't the endless ocean in which you were spawned back then, but only a narrow rivulet, trickling away into the desert..."

"You're wrong about that," I said. "I mean, yes, time flies by now, but it's not true that you seem like..." I heard a small break in my voice, paused to allow the unexpected surge of emotion to subside, and began again: "You don't seem a small part of my life at all. I feel more as if you've always been..." My voice trailed away.

For a moment, he said nothing, lowering his head. Then he raised his eyes to mine. "I didn't mean that, of course. And I'm...touched." He smiled gently. "I only meant to say that, as it is for persons, so it is for culture, at least in our time. That's what modernity is, really, isn't it? The world grown old. The experience of the world growing ever more compressed...condensed... time accelerating..."

"Well," I said after taking another swallow of my

coffee, "surely it was ever thus: *omnia mutantur et nos mutamur in illis.*"

"Oh, I don't mean simply change. Yes, of course, everything is always changing. You can't step twice in the same river and all that. Goodness, though, consider how much has changed in your life, and how much of that change has been far more rapid than any natural processes of cultural evolution in previous ages could ever be. I've heard you speak of it often enough — for instance, the decline of reading…how you were born in a time in which there was still a continuous tradition of literary experience, when it wasn't odd for a bookish lad like you to become captivated in his teens by Flaubert and Joyce, Proust and Nabokov…when university book stores actually sold books rather than sports paraphernalia, and students used to gather eagerly around the sale table to find cheap copies of, oh, Camus or George Eliot…when people could be seen carrying Signet or Bantam paperbacks of classic novels onto planes…"

"I may be idealizing the past a mite. One saw more Robert Ludlum than Dickens on planes."

"Even so, you've seen what at one time seemed a fixed feature of all developed cultures, and something you assumed would stretch on into an indefinite future — actual effective literacy — almost entirely extinguished in a handful of decades. Maybe not everyone was reading Tolstoy, but…"

"But even universal literacy was a late development in human history. Perhaps it was only an episode, taken in long perspective."

Roland smirked. "You know that isn't so. At least, it isn't true in principle, but only by happenstance. It's all the result of a particularly destructive technology — especially those horrid little oblong devices with luminous screens that everyone carries about — which a saner culture would never have allowed to work such devastation upon its young. And you some time ago fell far back on the track, and cultural change passed you by like a coursing whippet. You haven't lived in the 'objective' present — if there is such a thing — in all the years I've known you. You hate the culture around you with a ferocity so intense that it's inverted itself into almost total emotional lassitude... resignation."

I breathed deeply and attempted an amused smile. "I know you don't mean that as a reproach," I said, "but..."

"Oh, quite the opposite," he said. "I mean it as praise. Only a spiritual philistine could be at home in the world that's sprung up over the past few decades. And it's left you at liberty to pursue the winding paths of your own sensibility through the countryside and woodlands and along the shores of your own imagination. Surely you're glad that you have no desire to remain *à la mode*. I mean, for instance, you get to write in that polished antiquated style that gives you so much pleasure, and all you have to do is assume just enough of an ironic distance from what you're doing to get away with it."

"I like to think I'm more original than..."

"No, no," he continued, "I encourage you to keep at it. I say don't even bother beating on any longer, boat against the current; just surrender to the flow and let yourself be borne all the more swiftly and ceaselessly into the past. It's another country there, where they do things differently, but it's where you feel at home."

I laughed softly. "The number of — well, of *enjambed* literary references you can crowd into a few sentences is truly amazing."

He cocked an eyebrow at me. "Unlike your primate young these days, I actually still read. Anyway, the point is that this has been the story of modernity—this constant acceleration of experience—for a few centuries, and it's arriving now at a point past which nothing but the acceleration remains. You've achieved infinite speed, you poor monkeys, which is also a kind of paralysis, a kind of stagnation—pure velocity as pure stasis." He bent his head down and briefly nibbled at a toenail, then looked to the foot of the bed where the velvety surface of the counterpane was slowly growing more lustrous in the morning light. "What's the name of that digital broadsheet you publish again? *Leaves in the Mud? Leaves on the Pavement?*"

"*Leaves in the Wind*," I corrected.

"Oh, of course. A reference to Virgil I assume."

"Yes, very good."

"You've written something there about anacyclosis as I recall?"

"In passing, yes."

"Well, there you have a perfect model of what great cultural and social and political change meant in the minds of premodern persons. Yes, they knew that here below the moon all is vacillation, all is flux, but they also imagined that even amid the perpetual unrest of arising and perishing there was a kind of constancy…like the tides, ever changing yet ever the same, history was ever in motion but perpetually fixed within its appointed bounds and governed by its unvarying rhythms. Yes, too, they knew that human history swings from one order to another, but they believed that the structure of the world of *chronos* is periodic and reiterative, not merely serial. And yes, once again, there were great upheavals—the

occasional earthquake, now and then a Golden Horde
thundering out of the steppes to lay waste to Asia Minor,
every once in a while an 1848 — yet the perturbations
of the spheres came but rarely, with roughly the same
frequency as planetary syzygies, and once they'd passed
the perennial order was restored. Kingdoms fell, but
others arose to succeed them; empires rose but ultimately fell into dust; Alexander bestrides the world
like a colossus and then dies still in the flower of his
youth, Caesar conquers only to be unceremoniously
slain by small coterie of 'concerned citizens' solicitous
for the public weal; yet conquerors and empires, it was
assumed, would be ever with us. Stability amid change
was established by recurrence. It was possible to believe
in...*substance*, in something enduring, even unchang-
ing. It was also possible to believe in a profound unity
of nature and history — in the certain orderliness of
the revolution of the seasons proper to both. Ancient
persons couldn't visit museums, as you can, and stroll
through funereal galleries of vestiges and fragments
and echoes from the profoundest past, and consort
with the ghosts of vanished civilizations, but they still
had a sense of deep time. You see, Fortuna's wheel still
rolled along at the pace of a massive millstone in those
days, which may have ground exceeding fine, but could
do so only slowly. And so human beings had time for
contemplation, at least...time for reflection. They could
muse upon the passing years, the passing ages, and still
find themselves at home in the earth, upborne by her
enduring constancies."

I emptied my cup with a particularly deep swallow,
enjoying the bitterness of the soft sabulous dregs, and
then said, "I may be losing the thread again."

Roland sighed quietly. "Yesterday you were listening to Richard Strauss, weren't you? The *Metamorphosen*?"

"Yes, I was," I said. "Dohnányi and the Wiener Philharmoniker. It's a wonderful performance."

"And an exquisitely appropriate piece given what we're talking about. You know, a Japanese peasant during the Heian epoch and a Japanese peasant during the Sengoku period lived in very much the same world — even if the latter was slightly more likely to be killed by a wandering *ronin*. Think of Strauss, though. When was he born? 1864, was it?"

"That sounds right."

"And he died in 1949, if I recall. How amazing. He was born into a world of horse-drawn carriages in a time before the German nation even existed. He died in the aftermath of nuclear explosions in a time when Germany once more didn't really exist, as it had been partitioned among the allies. That's what it is to be modern. One outlives one's world. In fact, one outlives many worlds. And, as the years go on, the speed with which one world succeeds another continually increases. In the virtual age, culture itself dissolves into technology. The world that's coming — the worlds that are coming, rather, won't permit that reflective lapse of time, that contemplative distance I was talking about..." He fell silent for a moment, stared away into space, murmured something to himself, and then spoke aloud again. "No living thing possesses the spiritual or the neurological capacity to remain...to remain intact in such a world. The generations raised on the internet and social media won't be able to sustain their attention long enough to be able to read or speak or think. No time for the Dao, or for Romantic idylls...no time for the way of heaven or the mysterious poetry of nature. No time at all. Just infinite speed. At your back you can't even hear time's wingèd chariot hurrying near because it's always already raced on ahead of you and you can't catch up to it. The future now arrives in a dazzling and meaningless and disconnected stream of fragmentary experiences, all of them stillborn, all of them already dead and surpassed before they even speed into and out of view. And they never return because they never coalesce into anything that *could* return. The present is already hopelessly past. There'll be nothing so stable as mere anacyclosis in the future, I tell you. The dream of the turning spheres, of Fortuna's wheel, of the fluctuations of the tides of history, of the recurrences of the Platonic Great Year with all its embedded epicycles—none of that can survive into the cybernetic future." He fell silent again.

"Your mood seems unusually gloomy this morning," I remarked after a few seconds.

He appeared not to have heard me, but he did resume speaking. "And those poor, poor primates, they simply haven't the spiritual resources to resist. Their humanity is melting away into that virtual space. They'll just be part of the cybernetic system of production and consumption, hurtling toward an ecological and cultural collapse they won't know how to avert. All to serve the omnivorous monster—capitalism—which can't create but can only produce, and can't produce except by destroying, since ultimately destruction is its final cause. It's the reign of death in all things...the metabolism of life into lifeless wealth...the crucifixion of the world.... Capitalism is the Great Beast, the Great Harlot, the Abomination of Desolation."

For several moments I was not sure how to reply. Then, somewhat weakly, I said, "You're waxing unusually apocalyptic."

"Mind you," he continued, half to himself, "when one talks about history, it's always really very difficult to make clear connections between cause and consequence, what with the mystery of intentional agency being so much a part of its twists and turns." He turned his eyes back to mine and stared into them searchingly. "So," he said, "what's your thinking on the principle of sufficient reason?"

"What?"

*To be continued…*

6

# Roland on the Principle of Sufficient Reason

## (ROLAND IN THE MORNING, PART 4)

"WHAT'S YOUR THINKING on the principle of sufficient reason?" Roland repeated. "Yes, I heard what you said," I replied. "I mean, why are you asking?"

"Oh…" He paused and took a long deep breath, held it for a moment, and then released it again slowly. "It's

related to the points I was making about the metaphysics of time, and about the mechanistic philosophy, as
well as my…my animadversions, let's say, regarding
analytic method. It just occurs to me that there's a
distinct tendency among Anglo-American philosophers and dabblers in philosophical issues to think
of the principle of sufficient reason principally as a
claim about causality in the narrow, modern sense.
Admittedly, even Leibniz talked that way at times, and
of course for him the rational authority of the sciences
was an issue of paramount importance. But it does
strike me as odd that there are so many who find it
difficult to recognize that reasons and causes—at least,
causes as we think of them now—are not necessarily
the same thing."

"Well, quite," I said.

"Oh, it's probably obvious to you, but it's not so to
everyone. I mean, not very long ago I heard a philosopher from Duke—Rosenstein, Rosenberg, Rosenfeld,
Rosenbaum…some blushful ruddy rhodonym of that
sort—anyway, I heard him in a debate claim that quantum mechanics demonstrates the falsity of the principle
of sufficient reason—which of course assumes quite
a lot, but let's ignore that—because particles appear
and disappear within quantum fields spontaneously,
or at least unpredictably…" He shook his head. "But
you get the point: for him, a sufficient reason is simply a causal history. It would never occur to him that
there might be a reason—a rationale—for something
that *suffices* to explain why it's so without that reason
necessarily being limited to a mechanically causal narrative alone. Perhaps the efficiency that brings about a
particular quantum fluctuation requires some formal

and final explanation in order for that fluctuation to be understood in its totality. I mean, assuming there aren't any of Bohm's hidden variables at work...or assuming that the statistical or stochastic predictability of such fluctuations within quantum fields doesn't qualify as a *sufficient* explanation without being *deterministic*..." He paused as if pondering this.

"I think that's an ambiguous concept of sufficiency," I said after a moment. "I think the prevailing view among analytic philosophers is that a properly sufficient reason is a proposition that exhaustively explains a conjunct proposition — in the case of an emergent particle's sudden appearance, why *this* event *here* and *now*, specifically, without any causal remainder."

"What annoys me," said Roland, "is that the principle's simply a self-evident truth about all contingent truths. By definition, no contingent truth possesses the rationale for its existence wholly within itself, and so there's some conjunctive reason for its truth. Nothing comes from nothing. Hume aside, nothing happens merely in inert juxtaposition to all other events, without rational connection to its conditions and antecedents and consequents. Of course, a little...a little *Aristotelian* subtlety might go a long way. The web of rational relations that specifies any substance or any event as *this* substance or *this* event has to be grasped in all its aetiological diversity if one is truly to arrive at a proper judgment regarding why it's so."

I drank some more of my coffee. "That's the issue, I suppose."

"Do you recall," he suddenly asked, turning his eyes to mine searchingly, "what your beloved Nabokov thought the most hideous word in the English language?"

I tried for a moment to recall, but nothing came to me and I shook my head.

"Naprapathy."

It took a few seconds for the syllables to coalesce into an actual word in my mind. "Really?" I asked. "That's…what? It's some kind of fraudulent therapy, isn't it? Some kind of 'holistic' method that's meant to cure illness by…?" I paused, still searching my memory.

"Yes?" asked Roland.

"Massage?"

"Something of the sort," he said. "Manipulation of joints and muscles."

I shrugged. "What does it have to do with—?"

"It's the word itself that interests me," Roland interrupted.

"Why exactly? In fact, what does it mean—etymologically, I mean? That's certainly not real Greek. Not like 'rhodonym,' for instance—which I assume you just came up with on the fly. I have to say, I thought it very witty."

"Precisely my point," he said. "Not the bit about my witty neologism, that is, but the bit about 'naprapathy.' It's not constructed from two Greek stems. '*Náprava*' is a Czech word, meaning something like 'correction' or 'adjustment.' The therapy's called what it is just by virtue of having been invented by some Czech, one we can assume who didn't have a very good classical education." He began to lick one of his front paws.

After a moment, I said, "All right. I'm not sure I see the point you're making, though."

"Isn't it obvious?"

I breathed deeply, hesitating to answer for fear of— once again—disappointing him with the sluggishness of my apprehension. Finally, though, I dropped my head and said, "Not to me, I'm afraid."

A small and perhaps slightly pitying smile appeared on his face. "Oh, I was just trying to think of a reality composed from parts so intrinsically disparate as to exhibit no inherently sufficient reason for their conjunction. A reality, I mean, that's the determinate result of causes that, in themselves, are utterly accidental. There's always a reason."

"I'm sorry, I'm not…" I tilted my head and looked more closely at his smile. "I see," I said: "you're being droll."

"Perish the thought. My point is that there's a very real ambiguity, isn't there, between modal ascriptions of necessity and contingency in regard to the various conjunct causes and effects in any chain of entailments. I mean, the relation may be utterly contingent in terms of rationales—it may be logically contingent, that is—but those same rationales, when reduced merely to concatenations of physical and circumstantial causes, look utterly deterministic. The difference between reasons and causes runs through the heart of every event… every true proposition."

"Oh," I said, "you mean—"

Roland lifted a paw for half a second to curtail my words. "What I mean—if you'll excuse me for saying it my own way—is that the distinction between contingency and necessity is a judgment about relations among finite things and occasions. And even then it's one of degree: even to adjudge something as necessary is, as often or not, a verdict regarding not logical but merely metaphysical necessity, or even only nomological necessity. And even those judgments

are only relative, and can be applied solely within the
web of relations toward which they're directed. But, if
you extricate yourself from that web, and see it as a
composed whole from some remote vantage — if you
rise up out of the welter and *bacchantische Taumel*
of contingent conjunctions...the orgies of secondary
causation..." He paused and briefly furrowed his brow.
"No, I can come up with a better metaphor than that."
Seconds later, arching an eyebrow triumphantly, he
said, "Ah, I've got it. If you should choose to slip free
from the rude tumultuous embraces of Heracleitos
and flee for repose to the encircling arms of Par-
menides, just so you can get a good night's sleep, what
you'll find is that all such judgments are, viewed from
the angle of that blissfully recumbent posture, neither right nor wrong, but merely category confusions.
If you could combine all the relative relations and
conjunctions and conditions of the entirety of finite
reality in such a way as to pass judgment upon the
whole not as a composite, considered mereologically,
but as a rational totality — the totality of all that is,
all reality as such — then you'd have already induced
a kind of modal collapse. You have no context in
which to judge whether relations of contingency or
necessity pertain either internally or externally to the
complete integrated structure of what the Schoolmen
used to call 'real relations.' In the former case, that
of the totality's internal relations, the catenations —
the *chains* — of entailments now appear to be utterly
unbreakable fetters, harder than adamant. In the latter
case, admittedly, you can of course ask whether that
totality is itself something necessary or contingent, but
what are you asking then? An ontological question

about why there's anything rather than nothing? Or a causal question about how *this* reality rather than another came about? But what are you asking then — in the latter case, I mean? Within the contextless context of such a question, are you demanding that the relationship between the absolute and the contingent be elucidated in terms that apply properly only to the reciprocal relationship — the reciprocal *pathos* — that exists only between two contingent 'conjuncts' (to use the analytic jargon)? How is that possible if, *for* the absolute, there's nothing other *than* the absolute — no reality more real than reality in its fullness — and so no real relation of the absolute *to* the contingent?"

I swallowed my coffee down to the dregs, reached behind me for the press, and emptied what remained in it into my cup. "You're going a bit fast for me," I said.

Roland nodded patiently. "The simian brain works at a somewhat slower rate of rotation than does the canine, I know. Something to do with the proportion of energy expended by the brain relative to the average lifespan of the organism, I imagine. You need to conserve your *vis essentialis* by a more — well, let's say, a more Saturnine exercise of your wits, whereas I enjoy the luxury of a more Mercurial, more fleet-footed process of ratiocination. Don't take it as a value-judgment, though. It's merely a matter of the homeostatic regulation of energy-expenditure within diverse organic systems. Trees think even more slowly than human beings do, if you can imagine that."

"Do they?"

Roland smiled at me again, in an affectionate but bemused way. "*Sancta simplicitas,*" he murmured.

"Anyway, all this occurs to me because I was thinking of those analytic philosophers who deny the validity of the principle of sufficient reason. Needless to say, I have small regard for such a position. As I say, I see the principle as a self-evident truth about any predicable reality in the realm of finite things. But these philosophers seem intent on denying the undeniable, in some cases out of a desire not to be caught on the horns of a fairly famous 'theistic' dilemma, in others out of sheer perversity of temperament. Some, as you know, phrase the matter entirely in terms of 'propositions,' as the analytic sect has a tragic propensity to do. The argument goes rather like this: All true propositions are either necessarily or contingently true; those that are contingently true are true by virtue of chains of conjunction with other *contingently* true propositions, since a necessary proposition cannot explain a contingent proposition without rendering that contingent proposition in fact necessary; imagine, however, that the whole set of all contingently true propositions has been combined into one immense conjunctive proposition in its own right; this too would require explanation by the conjunction of yet another true proposition; but, if that proposition is itself contingent, then it solves no problem, as it is nothing other than another conjunction within the total set and requires further explanation; if, however, it turns out to be necessary, then this erases the modal distinction altogether and renders all truths necessary." He shook his head dolefully. "So many confusions," he said, clearly to himself. "So many baseless assumptions."

Several seconds of silence ensued before I asked, "Is that all you were going to say?"

He lifted his head and looked at me. "My apologies. I was momentarily lost in thought. You notice, I hope, how curiously this way of arguing confines itself to the level of conjoined propositions but nevertheless covertly shifts the enigma toward the issue of the... toward what they, the analytical sorts, would call the existential qualifier. Why does this whole exist? And the only 'proposition,' if you will, that can answer the question is one that functions within the system of conjunctions. But that's precisely the whole point of the principle of sufficient reason, surely: that it *doesn't* concern either necessity of contingency in an absolute sense, but concerns only explanations at the level of real conjunctions. Notice also how it's assumed in the argument that the totality can be drawn into the logic of finite conjunctive relationships without suffering the logical disruption of a wholly different kind of modal disjunction: that between the whole of reality as such and individual real things, or between the absolute and the contingent. I know that analytic philosophers typically think only in terms of existential univocities — I mean, as I've said, that's why analytic philosophy is as a rule a method for avoiding thinking — but that's no excuse for failing to grasp simple frames of reference."

"I expect," I said, "that the issue for the philosophers you're talking about is God — the theistic dilemma you mentioned — and they're thinking of God as some deliberating subject who decides to create the world, and does so by choosing one...one huge conjunctive set of propositions out of an infinite landscape of possible such sets, and whether his decision is therefore necessary or...necessary or free."

Roland's smile broadened. "You *do* understand. I'm
so glad."

"I mean," I continued, "if one wants to deny that
the principle of sufficient reason proves the *existence*
of someone who performs that function—I mean,
some demiurgic psychological subject who exists in
a landscape of possibilities that exceeds his present
actuality—then the argument is sound enough, I suppose. It's just the old atheist cavil—'If God made the
world, who made God?'—in another register."

"Very good, *mon petit singe*," said Roland in a genuinely pleased tone of voice. "It would have taken a
poplar weeks to work that out. And, of course, the
argument suffers from all the same logical barbarisms
as the village atheist's taunt does. But, of course, that's
only why an atheist might want to deny the principle
of sufficient reason. There are believers who want to
deny it too, in part I suspect because they too—being
of the same analytical bent—think of God as just
the instantiation of some kind of general category
of being: there is one $x$ such that $x$ is God…or Mr
God, or Ms God, or what have you. And, because
they don't want God to be deprived of what they
consider the highest rational trait of a real being, libertarian freedom to choose arbitrarily, they don't want
the explanation for the existence of the world to be
traceable back to any kind of necessary cause…any
sort of necessary *proposition*. Mind you, that should
have no bearing on whether a contingent reality
requires a necessary reality to explain its reality. As
long as the issue isn't ontological but merely propositional—'this antecedent state of affairs provides
the rationale for this consequent state of affairs,' that

is — the traditional metaphysical arguments for God remain in place. But what has been exorcised from the picture is the spectre of a determinism within the will of God, lest his liberty to make purely deliberative choices be compromised. Of course, as you've written about in the past — with, admittedly, a little assistance from me, but with some genuine acuity of your own — libertarian freedom of that sort is a contradictory idea, and the notion of God as a deliberating subject literally choosing among alternatives as a matter of preference is a silly and degrading way of thinking about God…one that imports finite imperfections into the divine. But, again, analytic philosophers are what they are."

"Alas," I said with a quiet sigh.

"After all," said Roland, "the most famous version of the 'immense conjunctive proposition' argument against the principle comes from Peter van Inwagen, who's a Christian. He too says that, if one were to place all the contingent truths of the whole universe into a single set or gigantic conjunctive sentence, the principle of sufficient reason says there'd have to be some explanation for the truth of that proposition, but this explanation couldn't be a contingent truth as it would then have to be included in the set and so would have to explain itself, which is impossible; so it would have to be a necessary truth, and all its effects would have to be necessary too, and so the set of contingent truths would disappear and everything that exists or occurs happens to be necessary, which is obviously a distasteful conclusion to reach; thus no sufficient reason can be found for this immense conjunctive proposition, and so the principle is false.

I'm not sure why the distastefulness or intuitively unpersuasive nature of universal necessitation is supposed to be a good argument against the validity of the principle of sufficient reason, even if it were the correct conclusion to draw from the principle—which, mercifully, it's not. The principle might be true even if, from our finite perspective, things seem to be contingent. But that's all irrelevant."

"All right," I said.

"Of course, that all makes it sound like a version of the argument against the possibility of a set of all sets—there can't be a contingent set of all contingent things—and then a version that doesn't properly apply to the problem. Again, though, this doesn't affect the whole… I suppose I'll just call it the whole 'cosmological argument for God,' even though that's misleading. A set, after all, isn't a substance, but only a purely notional abstraction, which merely delimits a certain collection of similar things in an altogether neutral way. It's indeed perfectly true that a substance can't be the cause of some other substance upon which it's dependent; an object dependent upon the universe couldn't also be the cause of the universe without causing itself, which is of course impossible. But the relation between a set and its contents isn't one of causal dependency, and so it simply isn't true that the explanation for a set of facts can't be included among the items of that set. If on the stroke of noon I make a decision about my life that obliges me to make a dozen more decisions before an hour elapses, all in accord with my first decision, there now exists a set of the thirteen contingent decisions I made during lunch, the *sufficient* reason for which is the first

decision in that series. Why I made that first decision is another question altogether, admittedly; but
all sufficient explanations can always be traced back
indefinitely to logically prior reasons, until one arrives
at the first cause of all things. The question then is the
nature of that first cause, and whether it's genuinely
modally capable of being comprised in a set of modal
real relations."

"I see."

"And that consideration also makes me wonder
whether the immense conjunctive proposition at issue
really requires any external explanation at all for why
it's true. What is it, after all, but an inconceivably large
catalogue of truths whose explanations are already
contained within the huge causal description that
constitutes it? 'Janet slapped Henry because Henry
got fresh because Henry was raised badly because
his father was habitually debauched because...?' If
though, after all the causal connections in this vast
farraginous proposition have been accounted for, the
real issue turns out simply to be why it is that this
universe as a whole exists, and whether its first cause
is a necessary one, that still remains an issue of the
ontological dependency of the contingent on the absolute, unaltered by the truth or falsity of the principle
of sufficient reason. But that's not my real problem
with this sort of argument."

"No?" I said.

Roland yawned, again pensively licked his front
paws a few times, and then said, "No, my problem
is that it mistakes the chief strength of the principle of sufficient reason for a debilitating weakness.
It treats the threat of a modal collapse between the

necessary and the contingent as an irresoluble paradox that makes the principle incredible and incapable of saying anything about God. In fact, that collapse is precisely what makes the principle indubitable — as well as perhaps a nearly infallible argument for the reality of God...and of freedom too, while we're at it."

I felt my eyes widen. "Now you have me at your mercy," I said. "You have to give me your reason... your *sufficient* reason, rather, for saying that."

*To be continued...*

7

# Roland on God,
# Necessity, and Freedom

## (ROLAND IN THE MORNING, PART 5)

ROLAND PAUSED FOR several seconds, apparently composing himself before speaking. Then, in a measured tone, he said, "I just mean to say, first, that — again — the principle of sufficient reason is simply a self-evident truth. If it weren't, there would still be no meaningful way of saying as much, since any argument for or against it depends upon its indubitability. Any argument from logic — any argument that *this* is true or *this* is false — is an argument that there's a sufficient reason for affirming or denying the truth of something . . . that there's some truth that makes *this* truth true. But that's a trivial concern. Performative inconsistency is inevitable, since language isn't a pellucid medium of truth, but only a sort of cleaver we wield to separate the sublime immensity of everything-all-at-once into more easily manipulated portions. Real knowing, real understanding, is finally beyond words; here below the moon, in the land of unlikeness, our words and meanings can't quite align, and so we have to dance about between them, gesturing wildly now at the one now at the other but never reaching repose. No, my real problem with those who make arguments against the principle isn't their inconsistency but rather their obtuse failure to recognize it. All their claims depend upon a confusion between the question 'Why is this particular thing what it is?' and the very different question 'Why do things exist?' Both are queries regarding the sufficient reason for something, admittedly, but they don't obey the same logic — the same logic of necessity and contingency, I mean."

I noted with disappointment that I had less than half a cup of coffee left. "I do feel as if we're moving in circles, and a little more swiftly than I can quite keep up with. Just to spare me vertigo, could you tell me: that business about a set of thirteen decisions made before noon, or whatever it was — you're not saying that a contingent truth can be its own sufficient reason, are you?"

Roland ran his tongue over his nose pensively and then shook his head gently, in a somewhat tsk-tsking manner. "No, that wasn't my intention. I was simply trying to draw a distinction between a 'set' of conjunctive propositions, which is just an abstract and limited collection, and any sort of actual thing in its concreteness. A set, depending on its definition, can be self-explanatory as *that* set. The contents of the set don't need to be explained because they themselves are the explanation. One decision leads to twelve more, and so the set of thirteen decisions is explained sufficiently by the conjunctions it contains. Now, if one then asks about the sufficient reason for that first decision, then one is operating within a larger set, and it may be that such questions are interminable in extension; and so the set of all conjunctive truths may have to be infinite to be rational, or maybe the very concept of a total set of all conjunctive truths is just a logical nonsense, like a set of all sets. Still, at the level of the logic of particular sets, and how they're defined, there's no point at which the answer to any of those questions violates the principle that a true proposition can't explain itself. The issue never arises. Explaining why *this* set contains these conjuncts is no more complicated than pointing at those conjuncts and saying, 'That's the set we're talking about.'"

"All right, if you say so, but surely that's still not the issue."

Roland smiled. "No, it's not. But, you see, the traditional way of applying the principle of sufficient reason — not yet called by that name, of course — was something along the lines of Thomas Aquinas noting that, even if the cosmos had existed from everlasting and will continue to do so forever, that entire reality's essence still can't account for its existence, and so there must be an ontological cause that doesn't fall within the series of purely contingent truths."

I nodded. "Yes, true."

"But that's not what, say, Peter van Inwagen and these other critics of the principle are talking about. They're talking about something more like the reason for God choosing to create this world—this total set of conjunctive truths—rather than another. So they're asking about some large deliberating subject who, out of a landscape of countless possible worlds somehow beyond himself, chooses one or more worlds to make real. But that's a childish picture of God. It reduces the ontological question to yet another causal question of the sort appropriate to finite real relations among contingent realities. And it wouldn't really be the being of the world that such a God causes, except in the same secondary sense that, say, you cause the being of my breakfast when you confect it and place it in my dish." At this, Roland furrowed his brow and trained a penetrating gaze upon me. "By the way, I'm getting a mite peckish. Do you think you might be going downstairs in the near future?"

I looked down at my cup, sighed quietly to myself, and drank from it. The coffee was still hot, but not hot enough. "I'm almost finished."

Roland's gaze lingered on me a few moments longer, not quite reproachfully but not quite patiently either; then he shrugged and looked away toward the window again. "I still say it's a dangerous addiction, those seas of coffee you imbibe every morning. Anyway, you see my point: a supreme being who 'exists' in a larger context of existence, alongside countless possible worlds, and who might *choose* to actualize one or another, would himself be only a finite dependent being, one who possesses unrealized potentials within himself, and who there-fore would be impotent to explain his own existence. Even then, what would that prove about the principle of sufficient reason? If one thinks of freedom as purely libertarian in nature, then why shouldn't a choice be its own explanation? He chooses this because he chooses to do so, perhaps. Maybe there's a purely benign infinite regress in such freedom: he chooses because he chooses because he chooses, because he's chosen to choose, and chosen that choice as well, *in infinitum...*"

"But you don't believe that, of course," I said, "either about the nature of freedom or about the nature of God."

"No, of course not," said Roland with a scowl. "That's the sort of thinking one expects of analytic philosophers and squirrels and others of that kind. I don't believe in libertarian freedom in that sense; I think free choices are always made for reasons that compel volition, and those reasons are possible only under the canopy of a natural orientation of the will toward transcendental values, and...well, you've written on this yourself, so I'm not telling you anything you don't know."

I nodded.

"And I certainly don't think of God as some supreme being actually deliberating among options and then determining what he wants to do arbitrarily, or even for good reasons. There aren't reasons out there for God in addition to the infinite actuality and infinite goodness of the divine essence. God doesn't 'exist' in the way beings exist. But I'm not even sure that this great *agonizing* dilemma of whether the explanation for this great conjunctive proposition must be necessary or contingent is anything other than a confusion about how logical entailment works. Even if one thinks of that explanation as some 'choice' made by Mr or Ms God, it needn't be a choice to select one possible set of conjunctive truths in its totality as a predeterminate whole; one could think of it as a necessary choice to create other libertarian agencies whose further choices haven't been predetermined. But, again, I think all of that's just silly. The question of why there's anything at all simply isn't a question about a supreme being or about any kind of cause within a chain of causes. Yes, it's a question that presumes an ultimate sufficient reason, but not one that can be reduced to a calculus of contingent or necessary entailments. God is 'necessary' *in se*, of course, in the sense that his essence and his existence aren't distinguishable. But that's necessity of an entirely different kind."

Now I too turned my eyes to the window and the slanting tiers of pale light pouring in through its jalousies. "I think I know what you mean."

Apparently, though, Roland was not quite sure of this. "What I find odd about the whole argument — the argument against the principle, that is — is that it mistakes the chief strength of the principle for some sort of devastating weakness. It's quite bizarre. The ultimate upshot of asking why there's anything at all rather than nothing is that, properly considered, it obliges us to follow the chain of sufficient reason altogether beyond relations of conjunctive necessity and contingency to an absolute condition that transcends the very distinction. As no contingency possesses the rationale for its own

existence — as, that is, its essence and its existence aren't
one and the same — all the contingencies there are,
taken together, depend upon a necessary reality that
isn't just some 'necessitated' conjunctive truth. Trying
to avoid this conclusion — or simply failing to notice
it — by claiming that there might simply be brute facts
without rationale is so self-defeating that it doesn't even
rise to the level of honest nihilism. Rather than treating
the possibility of a modal collapse as some horrible
contradiction that thwarts the ambitions of reason,
we should embrace it as reason's highest discovery.
That's what makes the principle so very illuminating.
*Of course* there's a modal collapse — *in God*. That's what
the very word 'God' means: not a thing among other
things, not a discrete reality that has real, qualifying
relations with other finite realities. Modal definitions
apply properly to entailments among finite realities,
but not to the being of all reality as such."

"But…"

"Yes, indeed, questions about necessity and contingency in regard to conjunctive truths all terminate in a
paradox if you're looking for an answer that's both ultimate and yet also just another conjunctive truth among
the rest. That paradox isn't reason's defeat, though, but
rather its highest triumph. It's the recognition that there
must be an explanation that really *is* absolute, as the
logical regress of mere causal entailments is an infinite
series of infinite series, and so an impossibility in itself.
The answer must truly be a *coincidentia oppositorum*,
infinite and metaphysically simple. The whole of reality in its absolute aspect simply isn't a thing. But that
collapse isn't, as van Inwagen suggests, a collapse of
freedom into necessity; it's the collapse of all modality

as such — into an infinite reality absolved of all modal
distinction, of all real relation, because it's the ground
of all relations. Divine freedom isn't some mere finite
exercise of deliberating liberty, limited by possibilities
outside God. It's simply the whole of reality in utter,
unimpeded fullness, *actus purus*, free in the only true
sense: subject to no limit on its infinite power to be
all that God is...all that reality is...all that Being is.
Or, rather, let's say this: God is freely the ground of
all necessity, and necessarily the perfect freedom of
infinite Being. And there's no larger context in which
the distinction between the free and the necessary is
meaningful in regard to God."

"Yes, but..."

"Freedom and necessity in God are no more distinct
possibilities than are existence and essence."

"All right, but..."

"All explanation terminates in a real infinity of *act*.
But that modal collapse in the infinite tells us nothing about relations of contingency or necessity in the
realm of the finite. I admit that, from the Parmenidean
vantage, *sub specie aeternitatis*, you can certainly think
of God's necessary Being providing a kind of extended
necessity to the whole of finite reality, since from that
vantage everything simply is what it is, as I've noted
already. In that sense, God's necessity casts a kind of
crystallizing light of total entailment over the whole.
But that's still just a perspective, one beyond modal
judgments, and so it too doesn't say anything about
determinism or liberty among secondary causes, within
the web of contingencies. From within that web — within
that Heracleitean flux — judgments of necessity or contingency, metaphysical or logical, are still valid and true."

"All I wanted to say," I interjected somewhat more forcefully, turning my eyes to Roland again, "is that I agree with you, absolutely, as you know. But it's no good. You're not going to convince analytic philosophers who think in terms of a mere supreme being who just happens to 'exist' and who makes deliberative decisions...or philosophers who think of existence as just some sort of mysterious brute given, which doesn't require an ontological reduction to an absolute principle, to accept the rationality of—how to put it?—of relativizing necessary and contingent propositional modes in that way. They'll still think that all you're saying is that God and God's creation are determined by some sort of logical or causal necessity."

A small smile crossed Roland's face as he also turned his eyes back to me. "I know. They're basically polytheists who just happen to believe in one god rather than many. What was the term you coined for them some years back?"

"Monopolytheists," I said, with perhaps a slight note of prideful relish in my voice.

"Yes, I like that one. Much better than 'theistic personalists,' which is just ponderous. You're right, of course: the self-evident truth of the principle of sufficient reason should finally lead them to abandon that way of thinking...to free themselves from the irrationality of that picture. But they won't let it. They'll always reverse the deductive sequence and conclude instead that the principle itself—which is, of course, their only justification for believing any deliverance of reasoning in the first place—must be regarded as dubious, or plainly false. For them, apophaticism is just evasion. For them, there are just things, and only things, and existence isn't anything more troubling than the instantiation of a category in some particular — some $x$ whereby it becomes valid to say, 'There's an $x$ such that $x$ is-a-dog.' Nothing more."

I drank the last of my coffee, stared vacantly at the dark silt of fine grounds at the bottom of my cup for a moment, and asked, "Do all dogs ponder these kinds of things? I've never had any conversations with other dogs at all, so I don't really know how..." I trailed off with a hapless smile.

Roland sighed, somewhat histrionically. "Now, now, let's not generalize. Dogs are no more or less diverse in their opinions and interests than any other species of rational soul. But the things we've been discussing this morning wouldn't be topics of much canine discussion *en famille*, as it were, since to us what I've been saying to you is just a collection of obvious truths. Our own debates are, of course, of a somewhat more complicated kind, on a somewhat more elevated spiritual plane."

"Ah."

"I think I've explained to you," Roland said gently, "that direct communication between our kinds — mine and yours, that is — is dependent on a certain — well, let's say a certain oneiric aptitude rarely found in simians. It's not a high achievement of intellect or anything, but it's definitely rare — almost a kind of mental disorder...of a fortunate kind."

"I see."

"That's why I talk only ever to you."

I began to nod, but then a memory came floating up murkily from the depths of my mind. "Is that really so?" I asked after a moment. "I recently came across a picture I took of you and my nephew, oh, it must be something like nine years back, and it certainly looks to me like the two of you are deep in conversation. It even looks like you're soothingly trying to get him to pay attention to some important point."

For a few moments, Roland looked as if he too were casting his mind back to a distant memory. "Oh, yes," he finally said, "now that you mention it, I do recall. Yes, for a few moments he became…susceptible, let's say. Not entirely percipient, but somewhat less apish than usual, and something of what I was saying was getting through to him. I doubt he recalls it, since he's not a fully pathologically extreme oneirolept like you, but just then he was vulnerable and so receptive. He was going through one of his spells of melancholy and confusion, you see." Roland wagged his head sadly back and forth a few times. "Such a confused and wayward soul…seeking guidance but recalcitrant to wisdom. But I like to think I helped him past that particular episode of doubt. I do worry about him sometimes though. What's to come of him, the poor perishing primate?"

I set my cup aside. "I'm sure you were a great help to him," I said. "You always are to me. Shall we get breakfast?"

Roland nodded, rose, lightly shrugged off his cover, stretched first his front then his hind legs, and leaped down from the bed. "Bring mine to me in the little brick courtyard in the garden if you will. I want to check the sproutings in the growing pots Mama has there."

I rose as well. "May I join you there?"

"Yes," replied Roland as he trotted through the door into the corridor, "but let's talk of lighter things over our meal. I have a few theories, you see, on…"

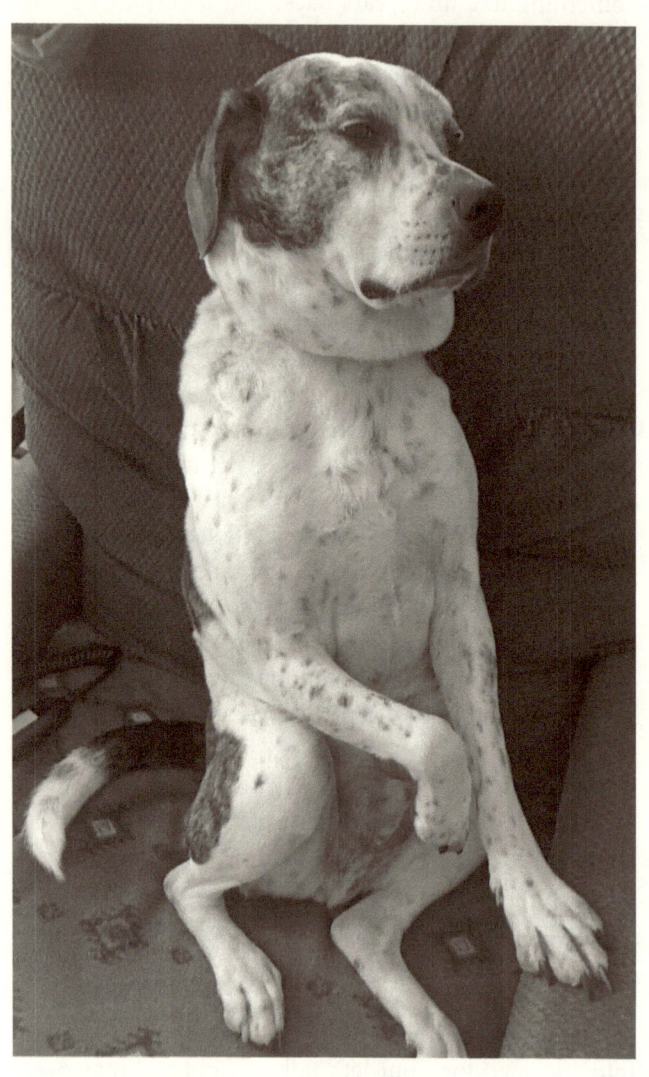

# Final Remarks on a Deeply Beloved Friend

## §1

Roland was fourteen years old when he passed away, in the early hours of May 13th, 2024. A goodly sum for a dog his size, but from a human perspective not nearly long enough. My son and I had returned from England the day before, where we had been for two weeks so that I could deliver a series of lectures at Cambridge. We got home in the evening. Roland greeted us ecstatically, he played with us for a bit in the garden, I gave him some of the special treats he likes, he spent the evening with me as I watched baseball, and we went to bed. Then, about half past three, he called out twice in a strange voice and was gone in an instant. He was lying beside my wife when it happened, his happiest place. He suffered no long decline in health, and his passing was very quick. That is some consolation, but not much. The grief is with us still. I believe he waited for my son and me to come home again before taking his leave. It is touching to me that he did so, and I am grateful for it, but it is painful as well.

I love him so very deeply.

## §2

I have never read a book by Robert Spaemann, despite his resplendent reputation and his undoubted genius, and I never will. My reason for this is entirely petulant, but my resolve is absolute. You see, many years ago — probably more than twenty-five — I bought a copy of *Personen: Versuche über den Unterschied zwischen »etwas« und »jemand«* and, on getting home, began flipping through it. Fate, however, immediately thrust her mischievous index-finger into the fluttering pages and called my attention to a passage in which Spaemann was explaining why animals do not qualify as persons. I admit, I have no idea whether Spaemann would really have considered an animal merely an *etwas* rather than a *jemand*, but those were the only two categories mentioned in the book's subtitle; but it would not have really mattered to me whether or not he considered cats and canaries, dogs and dolphins, and all the rest to be *bloße Dinge*. He had said enough. I tossed the book aside and never bothered to look at it again. I have known a great many animals over the years, and know that each of them has possessed a distinct personality and character, and I find it impossible to believe that any degree of personality can exist in the absence of personhood — at least, in any sense I would be willing to give the term. And it would have seemed to me to be a betrayal of the memories of all those departed friends to tolerate the moral obtuseness of anyone who would deny any of them the dignity of a distinct *jemand*. (Yes, yes, I know: Spaemann was a brilliant, civilized, and deeply humane thinker, and he was revered by many whom I respect. But — after all — there are enough of those in the world that I can survive the absence of his books on my shelves, and there is no such thing as an indispensable religious philosopher in the way that, for instance, there are indispensable poets.)

## §3

Petulant, as I say, but I happen to think I can summon up a metaphysical rationale or two to justify my reaction. I believe personhood to be a primordial truth about the structure of all reality, that all finite personality participates and expresses that divine ground, and that every individual "substance" comes to manifestation as a revelation of that original "I Am". Had I but world enough and time, I might dilate at enormous length on these claims. I have not and I will not; but I will note that this vision of things is one I find not only immediately attractive, but immediately convincing: it seems to me almost self-evidently true that our minds and the world about us are open to one another precisely because they both together subsist in a single principle of "personal" relation, and that all real being is essentially an act of "personal" communication, and that personhood as we know it in ourselves is not a final or (at any rate) *eventual* issue of some sort of pre-personal ontological ferment, but rather one expression among many of reality's deepest foundation. On the whole, as I have explained at tedious length in many places, I do not believe in "strong emergence" of any kind. Everything is always already "personal" — always already a particular act of expression seeking a response — and you can relate to nothing at all in any proper sense except as a spiritual commerce between, as Plotinus put it, "the divine within you" and "the divine within the All."

§ 4

My brother Addison sent me this not long after Roland's
passing:

> Does man alone possess immortality? The
> great words: "Behold, I make all things new"
> are certainly related not to man only, but to
> all creation, to every creature. We have already
> said that the spirit of animals, even the small-
> est part of it, cannot be mortal, for it is from
> the Holy Spirit…. In the new Jerusalem, the
> new universe, there will be a place for the
> animals, too…. Eternal life for [non-human]
> creatures will be only quiet happiness and
> enjoyment of the new radiant nature full of
> light, in communication with man, who will
> no longer torture and exterminate it.
>                 —St. Luke of Simferopol (Luke
>                 Voyno-Yasenetsky, 1877–1961)

Scripture seems to concur, for what it is worth.
Nowhere does it promise an afterlife or an eschaton
of disembodied — or, for that matter, reembodied —
souls floating in God's empyrean forever; rather, and
repeatedly, it depicts the Age to Come as a fully restored
and glorified cosmos, a new creation with a new sky
and a new earth, full of animal life of every kind. Oh,
but what does scripture know?

One of the reasons (among many millions) that I
find some of the very worst doctrinaire Thomists often
insufferable is not only that they adhere fanatically to
one of the most morally and imaginatively stultifying
eschatologies ever to have corrupted the religious consciousness of the human race; they positively revel in

it. Some years ago, a few Dominican wags at a fairly prominent institution associated with the order (I will not name it, but will merely note that it is located in DC and is what one might call a "house of studies") commissioned a set of coffee mugs bearing the motto "Your dog isn't going to heaven." They were disturbed, you see, by rumors of faithful but overly sentimental Catholics who perversely fail to assent to the Thomistic teaching that, in the Age to Come, the whole material cosmos — mineral, vegetal, and animal — will be utterly annihilated and, among material natures, only humankind will enter into eternity (either in bliss or in torment). Now, as scarcely need be said to anyone who has ever made even a cursory reading of scripture (a category, admittedly, that excludes many Thomists), and as I have just said, every single eschatological promise in the Bible concerns every kind of living thing; salvation is cosmic or it is nothing. Whenever, though, I have pointed this out to Thomist interlocutors in the past the response has always been that all that scriptural language about the creatures of land, air, and sea rejoicing upon a new earth, under a new sky, as well as all that nonsense about creation's glorification, and so on and forth — all of it, that is, is merely a conventional collection of fetching figural tropes; all it really means is that all the material elements of creation will be present in the final beatific state of the elect, in the purified distillate of their resurrected bodies. This, you see, is the rule with a great many Thomists: the ultimate standard of truth is *quod Thomas dixit*; and, if either scripture or tradition fails to comply with that standard, it is scripture or tradition that is wrong. That, though, is as may be; what bothers me about the aforementioned coffee

mugs is not that they represented bad theology, but
that they gave such eloquent expression to essentially
deformed souls. Those who commissioned the mugs
are perfectly free, of course, to believe that the souls
of animals—the "forms of animal bodies," that is—are
intrinsically mortal, and that God's moral nature is as
impoverished as their own, but it is altogether abhorrent
for them to delight in the thought, or to be so spiteful
as to amuse themselves by trying to torment those who
have lost pets with vicious little quips. I am entirely
unable to grasp what sort of pleasure can possibly be
extracted from trying to make children cry. Now, I do
not for a moment want to suggest that those particular
*Torquemadas manqués* are typical of all Dominicans; I
have known quite a few friars of admirable character
(and immaculate ordinal pinafores). Still, it all goes
some considerable way toward confirming me in my
prejudice that Thomism of the purest persuasion is
in certain cases not so much a personal philosophy
as a personal psychopathology. So much of its vision
of reality—of ultimate reality, in fact—is so pitilessly
and crushingly cold and bleak that it cannot possibly
appeal to a fully healthy mind.

§ 5

I am going astray here. Strong emotions too often
inspire strong language. So let me return to my earlier point.

One does not really require a metaphysics of personhood (or "personeity," as Coleridge would say) to
grasp that animals are persons—"someones" not merely
"somethings." One knows it merely from direct acquain-
tance. As I say, it is simply meaningless to suggest that

personality can exist in the absence of personhood, and only a moral imbecile could have any prolonged experience of animals and not perceive that each possesses a distinct character and personal nature. When I think of Roland, I remember countless typically canine behaviors, but just as many delightful eccentricities — not merely odd capacities, but startling idiosyncrasies of taste and temperament, and even of humor. He was a mimic, for one thing, and could reproduce human phrases with uncanny accuracy, but he also knew how to use those phrases in context: when, for instance, he very precisely emitted the syllables "How are you?" — and believe me, it was clarion-clear — he did so always and only to greet someone; when he wanted to get my wife's attention, his "Mama" had a bell-like and insistent quality to it; and, while he could not quite master the initial hard "c" in "Come along," whenever he uttered the words he turned about and began firmly to lead us where he wanted us to go. There were roughly two-dozen such phrases in his repertoire (and who can say how many others, spoken in canine, that we were too stupid to understand). Yes, of course, he had learned to associate certain sounds with certain behaviors; but that is how *we* learn language too. What distinguishes such associations as actual *linguistic* acts is the degree of intention or expectation with which they are employed.

In fact, he was in many ways a very talkative person. Another of those idiosyncrasies of his was the habit of joining in our conversations by seating himself human-fashion in an armchair and chiming in every now and again, whenever something occurred to him. It was much the same pose he liked to adopt when watching nature documentaries about wolves (I am not making that up). And he could communicate his feelings in any number of other, non-verbal ways as well, such as that calculated look of skeptical disappointment, and then the longanimous sigh he would eventually heave, when he was not best pleased by the dinner I had served him. Or the mirth he exuded when he was doing something he thought especially clever. And he had a thousand different looks with which to convey his jealous devotion to my wife when anyone had the temerity to attempt to divert her attention from him.

I should not continue, though. My eyes keep filling with tears. And that, of course, is the most irrefutable evidence of all that our relations with animals are relations with other persons. One can regret the loss of *something*, and even regret it keenly and for many years, but one can feel grief only at the loss of *someone*. There was someone there; and "someone there" is, to my mind, all that is required for the status of "person."

## §6

I do not feel in the least self-conscious about my grief over Roland's death. I know that he was a dog who lived a long and happy life, who died full of years without suffering any long lingering illness beforehand, and who left this life while lying beside the person he most loved in this world. I am enduring nothing comparable to what someone who has lost a child or a spouse goes through. That said, I freely admit that my sense of desolation is every bit as intense as it might be over the loss of a close human friend. But I am quite certain that neither love nor grief can ever be excessive; each is its own absolute measure, and knows its own proper proportions. And, as a rule, we generally fail to love or grieve nearly as much as we ought to do.

I should, incidentally, thank the many persons who sent condolences to me and my family in the days following Roland's passing. There were too many messages for me to respond to each individually. Someone remarked to me that many who expressed a personal sense of loss were grieving over the passing not so much of my pet dog as of the eponymous protagonist of *Roland in Moonlight*; but I do not see this as an either-or. I cannot really explain this, but I honestly believe that the Roland who used to go for at least two walks with me every day really was somehow present in, and genuinely gave shape to, the Roland of the book. I would not have written the book at all, in fact, but for the effect his personality had on me. Neither, for that matter, would I have written *The Experience of God*, at least in the way I did, but for his influence on me (my mention of him on the acknowledgments page was perfectly in earnest). And, now that I come to think of it, at least two of the stories in *Prisms, Veils* would not have occurred to me but for his presence (again, however, I cannot explain). *Cor ad cor loquitur*, and all that. *Spiritus ad spiritum*.

There are too many memories, though. And, in any event, all the anecdotes and reminiscences in the world can never suffice to convey any real knowledge of a living personality secondhand. All one can do by the attempt to do so is to hold oneself fast within one's own grief. Love is ineffable, and so is personality; and so our very inability to give voice to either is irrefutable proof that both are real. As long as Roland was alive, wherever our shifting fortunes carried us as a family, something of that paradisal happiness we knew up on the mountain where he spent his puppyhood remained with us, in the close circle of our life together. Now that he is gone, at least for a little while, that abandoned Eden seems ever more remote and barred by a flaming sword against our return. But the new sky and the new earth are still promised, and all our memories of Roland tell us why they are still worth hoping for and believing in. Somewhere, we have to believe, he is waiting for us.

# ABOUT THE AUTHOR(S)

David Bentley Hart writes on a great many topics in a variety of genres, producing works of philosophy, fiction, religious studies, theology, cultural commentary, literary criticism, treatments of the arts and sciences, and the occasional screed. His most recent books are *All Things Are Full of Gods: The Mysteries of Mind and Life* (Yale) and *Prisms, Veils: A Book of Fables* (Notre Dame).

Roland 婆 Hart was a dog, a polymath, and in all likelihood a saint or bodhisattva, who was boundlessly generous in imparting his wisdom to those most in need of it, and whose presence was always a source of unalloyed joy for those who loved him.